Secrets We Keep

Roberta Sharp

Contents

Chapter 1

It didn't matter how prepared Charlotte was for the talk, she dreaded the question yet to come.

"Do you want to keep the baby?" Sandy asked tentatively, eyes fixed on her best friend's pregnancy record book in her hand.

Charlotte glanced down at her belly that was hidden under her maroon hoodie. Last week, she didn't know that there was a bun snuggling inside her womb, depending on her for life. Today, after the doctor confirmed that she was twelve weeks pregnant, her world had instantly turned upside down.

"I don't know," she replied, almost whispering.

Charlotte wanted to do so many things in her life. She loved to challenge herself, she was thrilled to try stuff most people wouldn't, and she was open to exploring the morally grey area because she hated to limit herself. Her bucket list ideas about what to do before she died were getting longer and longer, but having a baby was none of them.

"It's not too late if you want to abort it," Sandy mumbled, sounding uncertain with her own idea. "I mean, it was conceived in one drunken night which you don't know who the father is. Plus, you'd been drinking until last week. You stopped when you suspected you were pregnant. And I'm no expert, but I heard that carrying a baby in your last year at college is hard, especially when the father isn't in the picture. Those are valid reasons, right?"

Charlotte pursed her lips, considering her best friend's advice while trying to see all the possibilities. "Maybe I can go back to that frat house and ask around? Maybe I can find that motherfucker."

Sandy raised her eyebrows. "Ask around how? Something like, 'Hey, do you guys know the guy I fucked three months back in one of your parties?'" She scoffed. "Do you even remember what he looks like? His hair color? His name?"

"No, not really." Charlotte sighed before throwing herself backward onto Sandy's bed. "I do remember his eyes, though. It's green, emerald green. And he has dark hair."

"Dark as in black or dark brown?"

"I'm not sure. The room was too dark to notice those trivial things."

"Any recollection of his name? Nickname maybe?"

Charlotte knitted her eyebrows, trying to remember anything that might be useful from that night, and she shook her head.

"Whose name did you scream when you had an orgasm then? Don't tell me you moaned Ethan's name."

Charlotte shot her friend a glare that could freeze a dragon's throat. "Can we not discuss my orgasm now? A more important matter needs to be addressed. Urgently."

Sandy put her hands in the air. "Sorry. I was just curious. How could you not remember anything about the guy you banged all night."

"I was drunk! It was the night Ethan broke up with me. I was so lost and in need of cock," Charlotte replied, wincing inwardly after listening to her own answer.

"You got one alright, and you've got the bonus, too. There." Sandy pointed at her belly.

Charlotte groaned as she put both her hands over her face. "I swear we used a fucking condom that night. That rubbish," she cursed under her breath.

"Are you sure it's not Ethan's?"

"I'm sure as hell. We hadn't had sex for weeks when we broke up. If it was his, I would've been four months preggo."

Sandy nodded but a frown grows on her face. "Seriously though, even if you find him, what are you going to say to him?"

"That we are pregnant? Maybe we can figure out what to do together?" Charlotte knew she sounded like the dumbest person who existed at that point. Or maybe she could blame it on her pregnancy brain.

"We? There is no we. You two aren't a couple. And what makes you think he remembers you?" Sandy pushed further, earning a shrug from her friend. "If he remembers you and what happened that night, he will easily say 'abort it'. If he doesn't recognize you, he will think you're a mad girl who is desperately in need of a random guy to father her child."

Charlotte let out a painful moan. She hated it when Sandy was right.

The scene of the wild party flashed in her head. She was so pissed and disappointed with Ethan that night because he chose to break up with her instead of working on their problems. She begged him to give her a chance to explain, but his mind was set. The next thing she knew, she agreed to Willy's offer to go to a frat party at his campus and forget about her shitty night.

'Never go to a frat party and drink your ass off after a messy breakup'. Charlotte wished she'd listened to this piece of advice, but she didn't. As the night wore on, she kept dancing her pain away and chugging down any alcohol within her reach. Luckily, she didn't puke from too much drinking, but she did get horny. Very horny. Her lucky stars seemed to shine so brightly when she bumped into a hot dark-haired guy with a pair of mesmerizing green eyes. Just what she needed, he was at the same stage as she was: drunk and eager to fuck.

One thing led to another and in the next thirty minutes, they ended up in one of the empty bedrooms, playing hide the sausage. It was bliss. Despite how much she wanted Ethan back that night, this guy helped her numb the stinging pain from the fresh break-up for a while. At least until she woke up the next morning, naked, with a painful hangover, and a stranger sleeping next to her, also unclothed.

She got dressed and ran.

Charlotte groaned again from the memory before rolling herself to the side, burying her face in Sandy's fluffy throw. "What am I going to do?" she asked helplessly.

"I would think terminating the pregnancy is a wise choice right now."

"I don't know, Sandy. I saw it on the ultrasound monitor this morning. It already looked like a real baby!" Charlotte whispered in horror. "I can't kill it, or that image will keep burning into my head for the rest of my life."

"So, you want to keep it," Sandy concluded for her, but she couldn't confirm it either.

Instead, she muttered softly, "My parents will kill me."

Sandy, who was always on the rational side, stared at her with sympathy, almost pitying her; the look that her best friend always gave her every time she screwed up and she hated it. Because she always screwed up. She didn't need a reminder from anyone else that her life was a mess. A gigantic ball of mess.

"If you want to keep it, you need to figure out how to break the news to them sooner or later," Sandy said matter-of-fact-ly. "The sooner the better."

"I know," Charlotte grunted. "They will be livid for sure. It'll prove them right that I'm still the impulsive girl who never learns and has no reservations for her future."

Sandy stood up from her chair and sat next to her best friend. She ran her fingers through Charlotte's brown lock that partly covered her face, brushing it backward gently. "You might be a little bit impulsive but what I see from you is a brave, open-minded, and non-judgmental person. And you give a fucking damn about your future. Don't let their words get in your head."

Charlotte squeezed Sandy's hand that was still on her hair and smiled. "You always know how to make me feel better."

"And you know that whatever decision you make, I will support you. If you want to terminate it, I will be there during the whole process. If you want to keep it, I'll help however I can until the delivery time comes."

Thinking about the labor was enough to make Charlotte's stomach twist. It felt like her vision of life ended when her water broke. She couldn't think of anything further than that because it was too terrifying to picture. Once realizing that she would have to deal with it in six months if the baby arrived on time, she shivered. "How will I raise the baby?"

Sandy frowned. "Huh? Do you want to raise the baby your-self? I thought..."

"I would give it away?" Charlotte finished Sandy's line, feel-ing a small jab in her chest.

Sandy nodded. "I thought you wanted to keep it because you just didn't have the heart to kill it," she said, slightly confused. "You don't want it in the first place, right? I mean, after the baby is born, you can make another family happy with their new little bundle, and you can move on with your life."

Ignoring the unsettling feeling that grew in her, Charlotte had to agree that Sandy was right. Her life might be put on pause at that very moment, but she could move on after making sure the baby was in good hands. Because she de-served a future too, hopefully with Ethan back in the picture.

Charlotte forced a smile. "I guess I can do that."

Chapter 2

Monday morning is my worst enemy. I don't want to say goodbye to my blissful weekend, I hate to go back to my chores after having a super lazy Sunday, and I loathe this stupid traffic. But with another human being sitting in my backseat and needing to be at school in fifteen minutes, I have no choice but to dip my butt into this craziness.

Sitting in the driver's seat, I lean forward with my fingers clutching the steering wheel. My eyes are fixed on the traffic light, wishing I could burn it down with an invisible laser light coming out of my brown pupils. We've been stuck at this intersection for a good twenty minutes, and the freaking light turns green only for fifteen seconds before switching back to red. I swear I will sue the person who made this rule.

To add to that, my seven-year-old daughter hasn't stopped chirping since she woke up this morning, prompting me to bite the inner part of my cheek to refrain from snapping at her.

"Diana and Robby kissed last week," Chloe says. "Does it mean Robby is Diana's boyfriend now?"

"Uh..." I drum my fingers on the steering wheel, trying to recall any conversations with my sister about her daughter having a boyfriend. Nothing comes up. "Can be. What did Diana say about it?"

"Well, Robby never really said they are a couple but Diana thinks that they are."

"Oh." The green light blinks. I grab the stick and shift, ready to hit the accelerator but the red mini cooper in front of me doesn't move its ass fast enough. "Come on, come on, come on, you turtle!" The orange light flickers and right after the car passes the line, the red light returns. I throw my hands in the air and cuss, "Dammit! You gotta be kidding me!"

"Calm down, Mama."

I grit my teeth. "We're late, honey."

"I know, but swearing is unnecessary."

Shit. I gulp down a fake lump in my throat, having a taste of my own medicine. She just repeated the very line I said to her every time people cursed in front of us. I sigh. "You're right. Sorry. That was unnecessary."

"So, do you think they are boyfriend and girlfriend now?"

Here we go again. She will not drop the topic until she says so. "I can't answer that question, to be honest, but if they have kissed like what you said, they probably are."

Children nowadays are nothing like what I knew back in the day. I don't know if I wanted to laugh or cry when I learned that kids at Chloe's school were already familiar with the idea of dating and kissing. Some of them even went home with plastic bands wrapping their fingers and proclaimed that they were married! It's just a puppy love thing and it's harmless, but it's enough to give me a headache when my daughter shoots random questions now and then. Especially when I suck at that department.

"Mrs. Donegal kissed the gardener but they are not a couple."

My breath hitches in my throat. "What?"

"Mrs. Donegal kissed Mathew but they are not a couple," Chloe repeats her line, slower with more pressure in her tone as if I'm too dumb to understand her.

"Yeah, I heard that," I reply, shifting my gaze to her in the rear-view mirror. "But how did you even know about this? Did they do that in the open?"

"No." She frowns but then her eyes widen. She lets out a soft gasp as she brings her hand to cover her mouth.

I peer at her. "Chloe Ann Garnett, did you use the telescope to spy on our neighbors?"

My daughter winces before reluctantly lifting her gaze to look back at me, a regret coating her eyes. "It was an accident! I didn't mean to spy. I was just cleaning it up and peeking through it to check if the lenses were clear enough, and...I saw them."

I take a deep breath as I massage my temple. "You know the rule, young lady. No telescope for a week."

"But I didn't do it on purpose, Mama. It really was an accident!"

"It doesn't matter. You broke the rule, so you need to hand it to me tonight. End of discussion."

My daughter grunts in the backseat but she doesn't dare to say anything further, which is smart of her. We've agreed about this before. Since she'd developed an interest in astronomy and all the things happening in space, I bought her a good-quality children's telescope for her birthday gift six months ago which she loves to bits and pieces. However, there are rules that she needs to follow: regularly clean it by herself, and not use it to spy on neighbors.

The green light finally blinks again, granting permission for me to run my car at the maximum speed limit. But it's useless. A few hundred meters ahead, we are greeted by the same problem again. That's it. I'm done with this nonsense. I need to either move to the neighborhood closer to her school or transfer her to the school closer to our house.

This was never a problem before, but since they built the toll road across our town last year, the traffic hasn't been the same. To make it worse, the toll entrance is right between our house and Chloe's school. Every morning, cars are piling up on the street, waiting for their turn to pass the gate. And Monday is absolutely the worst.

At the next traffic light, Chloe still doesn't say a word. She's probably busy licking her wounds from getting her baby suspended for a week right now. I glance at the mirror to check on my daughter who is staring out of the window with a gloomy face. Feeling my chest tighten, I fight the temptation to reconsider my decision. This is one of the real struggles to become a parent: teaching your child lessons with a minimum degree of lenity. But as much as I don't want to see her sad, I need to be consistent with my words. She needs it.

I know she was telling the truth when she said it was an accident. But she also needs to learn that there are two kinds of accidents: the one you can prevent from happening, and the one you can't do anything to avoid. Hers definitely falls into the first category. She might not have done it on purpose but she also didn't keep in mind how important it was not to point the telescope lens at the neighbor's space. Hopefully, this suspension will help her remember it next time.

I clear my throat. "So, about Mrs. Donegal–" I pause a bit, observing her. "You're right. Some people kiss but they aren't necessarily a couple."

Chloe turns her head slowly, and her emerald green irises lock with mine. "Will Mr. Donegal be angry? Diana gets angry every time Robby plays with another girl."

"Pfft." I wrinkle my nose, thinking about the best answer I can come up with. "Maybe. Maybe not. Sometimes, adults do confusing stuff, but it's only confusing because we don't know the whole story behind it. Maybe Mr. Donegal knows about it and he doesn't mind. Maybe he doesn't know it and he will get angry when he finds out. But the thing is, it's not our problem to worry about."

Our car stops a few meters from Chloe's school entrance four minutes before her class starts. Once she manages to get out of her seat, she leans over to give me a quick kiss, not quite in a cheerful mood yet.

"Have fun at school, sweetie," I say as I beam at her. "And oh, what you saw in Mrs. Donegal's house is not something to discuss with someone else. Okay?"

"Okay," she mumbles.

After putting on her green knit hat, Chloe hops off the car and runs towards her school gate.

For the third time, I promise myself that I will never drive to my new workplace. It's located in the city which theoretically is only a thirty-minute drive from our place. Theoretically is the keyword because it only happens in the middle of the night. During rush hours, once I enter the city's inner ring, the traffic is pure evil. I make a mental note that I need to find a private school-bus service for Chloe so that I can take a train to work.

This is my second week joining Remington Group, a worldwide energy supplier company. After four years working in the construction & transport industry, I finally made my way through to an account executive position in this multi-billion dollar company. To be honest, I still can't believe that they see me fit to join their team; it feels surreal. It's probably pure luck, or maybe I deserve it —I don't know, but raising a kid on my own has slowed me down with my career path. Sometimes, it forced me to skip opportunities because of my situation as a single mom. Not that I regret it because Chloe is my priority.

I almost decided to let her go eight years ago, but the more she grew in my womb, the more I couldn't bear the thought of losing her. The fluttering, kicking, rolling, or even the rhythmic twitch of her hiccups inside my belly were the moments I waited eagerly for every day. When she was born, I was sold.

The first year of becoming a mom was hard. I had to take a break from university and focus on her, with my parents' help, of course. As expected, they weren't happy at all when I broke the news about my pregnancy, but they fell in love with Chloe instantly once she was born. I went back to school after Chloe was eight months old, determined that it was my turn to focus on the plan for my future that I had abandoned long enough. Little did I know that things would never be the same because Chloe had become a part of my future.

"Good morning, Ms. Garnett," greets a woman behind the receptionist desk as I enter the Remington building. She digs into a white box in front of her and pulls out a small blue card with a gold and yellow string attached to it. "Here is your ID card. You can use it as a building pass and access certain facilities. The details are stated on the backside of the card. Can I have your trainee pass back, please?"

"Sure." I hand her the ID card I used during the welcome training last week. "So, I go straight to the Knight and Co.'s floor today?" I ask after having a quick look at my new company ID card.

"Yes. It's on the fourth floor. You will be expected in the main meeting room."

"Oh?"

"They have a kick-off meeting every first Monday of the month. Everyone will be there and as a newcomer, you will be introduced to the whole team. Good luck!" She smiles at me like a toothpaste model.

"Right. Thanks" —I glance at her name tag— "Francesca." With that, I turn on my heels and make my way to the fourth floor.

Despite being employed by the Remington Group, I was hired for its subsidiary, Knight & Co., which exclusively handles the marketing and distribution work. After spending a few days on the welcome training and corporate introduction last week, my actual first working day has finally arrived. And I'm nervous as fuck.

Chapter 3

I left my steady job of five years for this company, which means I can get sacked during my six-month probation if I fail to deliver the required performance. If I'm out of a job, I will need to find another job as soon as possible to keep my bills covered. And if I'm too long in between jobs, I will have to make a few adjustments, and it will suck because I have a kid to raise. Talk about being nervous!

Okay, I'm exaggerating a bit. We do have savings to survive at least two years of not-so-extravagant life. Still, that money should stay exactly where it is now. Isn't that the very reason we call it savings? We need to keep it —increase the amount if possible— and try not to spend it, right?

The elevator stops on the fourth floor and the doors slide open. Once I walk out of the car, I'm welcomed by a compact yet cozy lobby with a big blue sign 'Knight & Co.' on the white granite wall behind the receptionist's desk. A pair of Gold Palms in yellow pots adorns the corners of the room, bringing in nature's vibe to balance the modern interior design.

There are corridors on either side of the company logo but I can't see anything else other than glass walls along the passageways.

A young woman, who I'm guessing is in her early twenties, sits behind the desk, talking on the phone while her eyes are fixed on the computer screen. She doesn't notice me walking in her direction until I stand right before her desk. She lifts her gaze and raises her forefinger to signal me that she won't take long.

I nod and step away, giving her room to finish whatever she's doing now. I shift on my legs as my fingers fiddle with my new ID card, eyes roaming over the lobby on the fourth level. It's when the elevator dings, and then the doors slide open again, revealing a woman around my age in a knee-length black dress wrapped in a fitted grey blazer. She's wearing black plain tights and nine centimeters stilettos that match the color of her suits. Her straight black hair is pulled into a ponytail, swaying gaily as she walks in my direction.

"Morning," she greets.

Not sure if it's addressed to me or the receptionist girl, I smile at her and greet her back, "Good morning."

She strides past me and the receptionist's desk, heading to the corridor on the left, but then she halts and turns around. "Are you...the new account executive who is starting today?" she asks, tilting her head as if she's trying to remember something. "Sharleen, right?"

"Yes, I am the new account executive," I reply with a wide smile, feeling a little less nervous for some reason. I take a few steps forward and extend my hand. "And it's Charlotte. A pleasure to meet you."

"Likewise. I'm Gina and we will be working together." She shakes my hand while shamelessly taking in my figure before her eyes dart back to meet mine. "Welcome on board. And let's go, the meeting is almost starting." With that, she turns around and begins to walk, leaving me no choice but to follow suit.

"Whoa, where are you guys going? You can't just bring her inside, Gina!" the receptionist girl asks in panic, her palm covering the phone receiver.

"Of course I can," Gina replies.

"But I need to have her name first! The last time I let in a woman who wasn't on the guest list, I almost got slaughtered alive!"

Gina spins around, giving the receptionist a deadpan look. "Girl, I'm making your life a tad bit easier. She's the new executive on my team, meaning she isn't our big boss' one-night stand, meaning her name is sitting on your list. I'm bringing her in."

Seeing how these two girls glare at each other, I clear my throat. "The name is Charlotte. Charlotte Garnett."

The receptionist quickly grabs a pen and jots down my name on her note. She glances at me while mouthing "thank you" before resuming talking to the person on the phone.

Realizing that Gina is already a few meters ahead, I jog to catch up but my eyes keep roaming over my surroundings. The corridor is not as narrow as it looked from the lobby earlier. A dark blue carpet sprawls along the passageways and glass walls run on either side of us covered by striped glass film. Judging from the absence of light in most rooms, I doubt that this side of the floor is the employees' working space. Faintly, I hear murmurs and hums coming from the far end of the corridor.

"Here's where all the meeting rooms are. Our working place is on the other side, but we don't have time to check it out now," Gina confirms my assumption. "We have a kick-off meeting every first Monday of the month, which is today, and you don't wanna be late for this." She stops at the last door of the hallway and glances at me. "Ready?"

"As ever," I lie, taking a deep breath and walking to the door that Gina is holding open for me.

The room is packed with people. Most of them are standing in groups, engaged in a serious discussion, or just talking in a relaxed manner. A few of them choose to sit alone, burying their faces in their gadget screens or just spacing out, not seeming that enthusiastic to embrace the day.

People don't freeze dramatically when Gina and I enter the room. They indeed take a second glance before continuing whatever they've been doing before I walk in. Perhaps seeing new faces isn't something uncommon for them. Does it mean that the company has a high rate of employee turnover? Or is it just me that doesn't look impressive enough when I make my first entrance? I glance down at my beige chiffon blouse and black pants to check if my outfit looks somewhat presentable.

It did this morning. But now I'm not so sure anymore.

These people are what you can call office fashionistas. Men are in suits or at least in branded dress shirts and pants, while women are wrapped in voguish business attire which screams professionalism and wealthiness. The mixed scent of expensive perfumes and men's aftershaves envelops the air around me. Is it because they want to impress their boss in the kick-off meeting or do they dress up like this every day? Compared to them, I look like a waitress who delivers a tray of drinks and snacks at a gathering party. I feel under-dressed.

Apparently, I'm still used to how things worked in my previous construction company, where people got dressed merely for practical purposes. As long as we didn't go to work in pajamas and covered the parts that needed to be covered, we were cool. Not that I'm against fashion trends. It's more the nature of business in my former workplace just didn't give me enough room to explore that. Plus, eighty percent of the population were male technicians. Hence, it explains my relationship with fashion.

Gina escorts me to one group that crams the spot at the front corner by the window. Two women are sitting on a table while two guys stand in front of them. I instantly spot Max, my direct boss who was involved in the screening interview during my recruitment.

"Hi, Charlotte. It's good to finally see you here! Welcome to the team!" Max greets me with a wide grin. He shakes my hand before introducing me to the rest of the team. The other guy is Sebastian, who has been on the team for four years. Before them are Shanti and Donna, the duo who handle the administration work for the team. Shanti has been with the company longer than Sebastian, while Donna just joined last year, around the same time as Gina. After a little chit-chat, Max and Sebastian are summoned by another team to discuss who knows what, leaving me with the girls.

"So, what's the meeting about?" I ask the girls.

Gina waves her hand with a dismissive gesture while her other hand is busy scrolling down her phone screen. "Boring stuff. We will give a recap about our last month's achievement and what's the plan for this month."

"But why does everyone have to be here? Why not just the managers? It saves more time."

"Oh, he wants to see all of us because he loves us too much, just as much as we love him," Shanti replies, followed by a giggle from Donna.

"He who?" I ask.

"You will see." Shanti beams before leaning into my ear. "He's the hottest creature in the building. Make sure you hold your knickers in place or they will drop on the floor when our daddy enters the room."

Gina snorts. "Wait until you have to talk to him, your panties will go back up by themselves, in one blink of an eye."

"He can be nasty sometimes, that's true. But still, he's my nasty daddy," Shanti says.

"Sometimes is the understatement of the year. He is always nasty. You will need to keep your blood pressure in check when he's around." Gina rolls her eyes. "Have you heard about his new assistant? He's not coming back today."

"Alex is leaving?" Donna chips in, a disappointment in her tone. "Who told you?"

"I have sources," Gina replies smugly, still not shifting her gaze from her phone. "So, he's assistant-less again today. Let's see how fast they can find a replacement."

"I don't mind going up and helping out," Shanti says dreamily.

"Over my dead body." Gina scoffs.

"What dead body?" Sebastian's voice comes from behind me. He then plops down between Shanti and Donna, earning protest groans from the pair as they have to scoot to both sides.

"It's about Mr. Knight's new assistant–"

"He is dead?" Sebastian's eyes widen.

"No! Stop cutting me!" Donna glares at Sebastian. "According to Gina, Mr. Knight's new executive assistant quit, again. And Shanti is more than happy to help out until they find his replacement."

"Not happening. Shan-shan stays with us," Sebastian replies before turning himself to face Shanti. "And what will you gain from that? You know he won't drop any penny for your service."

"He doesn't need to. I prefer that he drops something else, though." Shanti twirls a lock of her brown hair, her eyes blinking rapidly.

"Like what?"

"Like his Hugo Boss boxer."

Sebastian's nose wrinkles as his lips curl up. "Ew! How do you even know the brand of his underwear?"

"Oh, I know almost everything about him. Inside out. You have no idea."

"Enlighten me. What do you know about him that I don't?" Sebastian challenges before adding, "Except for his underwear brands. Or his condom size."

Shanti purses her lips, looking up at the ceiling. "That his balls are bigger than your brain?"

Donna practically screams while Gina snorts and makes a weird gurgling noise. And I'm in love with my team already.

"Poor Hugo Boss." Sebastian shakes his head while making a clicking noise with his tongue. "What has his underwear done to him to deserve all this?"

Shanti narrows her eyes at him. "It's an insult to your brain, you dimwit, not to his balls."

That's when the meeting door swings open, announcing the arrival of a man dressed in a dark grey Armani suit. Behind him, stands a middle-aged Asian man who looks equally intimidating as he is. The laughter, the hum of conversations, and the shuffling noise die down instantly.

"Good morning!" the man in a grey suit greets in his deep voice as he strides to the middle of the room. The fact that he shuts up everyone solely with his presence is evidence that he must be the number one person of Knight & Co., Our CEO.

I saw his picture during orientation week, but he looks younger in real life; he's probably in his mid-thirties. The way he carries himself screams arrogance, also a warning that he's not a man to fuck with. He's not extremely tall but definitely taller than average height. His chestnut hair is pulled backward in a slicked-back style, and his chiseled jaws are free from stubble. Unfortunately, I can't study his face since he's now standing in the middle of the room with his back to me. All I can see is his rear side and my eyes are stuck on his bottom for some reason.

The man with gigantic balls in Hugo Boss underwear. Okay, I shouldn't have that weird image in my mind but I can't help it. Shanti's words are tattooed in my mind already.

Mr. Knight rubs his palms in excitement. "I can feel everyone's enthusiasm about our first-trimester achievement. But before we go down to our sales figure" —he glances at the man who has been standing behind him— "our CFO, Mr. Tan, is going to share some vital information." After giving the floor to Mr. Tan, Mr. Knight heads to the closest table and sits down.

Now that he's facing in my direction, I can have a better look at him. He has pale skin. Even for the winter season like now, he is paler than most people. Probably life as a CEO takes away the luxury of having fun under the sun as normal people have. Still, it can't hide his hunkiness. His square and sharp jawlines frame his intense eyes, straight nose, and plump lips flawlessly. He's not bad. No, scratch that. He is hot. And it makes me wonder how pictures in the company profiles can be so deceiving.

Something inside me stirs. The more I look at him, the more my mind picks up the familiarity, but I can't pull the exact memory out of it. Probably I'd seen him in an online business journal way before I joined this company. He's one of those important people in the business society after all.

As if sensing that someone is gawking at him, Mr. Knight shifts his gaze, and his mesmerizing green eyes lock with mine.

My heart skips a beat.

Chapter 4

For over eight years, I've been wondering if I will ever see the pair of those emerald irises again before I die. Every time I met a guy with green eyes, my heart skipped a beat with anticipation. Still, none of them were the ones I saw at that frat party. Sandy and Sophie, my sister, always emphasize that I was drunk that night, and that my memory of Chloe's father is unreliable. But I know better. I still remember the exact shade of green they were and how intense his eyes were when he looked at me. It felt like he was piercing me and searching for my soul.

Just like what's happening right now.

Tearing my eyes from him, I look down and stare at my beige shoes as if they become the most interesting objects to observe on earth. Mr. Tan's voice is muffled by the dull thumping sound in my ears as my heart beats so hard against my chest.

This can't be true. He can't be him. This is just one of those moments where I get caught up in the prospect of meeting the ghost of my past. This is just like every other day when I bumped into a pair of green eyes. They are everywhere, aren't they?

Also, judging from his age, which is probably thirty-five or thirty-six now, he must have been around twenty-seven at the time I slept with Chloe's father. He was a bit too old to lurk around a wild frat party, wasn't he? Then no, he can't be him. But why can't I shake away the thought of him being connected to Chloe? Is it because I've seen him somewhere online that my mind plays tricks on me? Is it because of the familiarity?

The familiarity.

A realization dawns on me like a bucket of cold water. No, it's not because I've seen his picture somewhere before orientation week. It's because I see a glimpse of him every day through my daughter's face. The resemblance between Chloe to him is undeniable. Those eyes. That nose. Those lips.

No. No. No.

This is just a coincidence.

This is just one of those typical days. Tomorrow, I will bump into another man with a pair of piercing emerald-green eyes that throws me back to the memory of that party. Because they are everywhere. Yes, Chloe's father is everywhere but here.

I've been sucked in by my thoughts when Gina pokes my waist with her elbow softly. I instantly turn my head to her but before I open my mouth to ask, I feel pairs of eyes on me. Scratch that. All eyes in this freaking meeting room are on me right now. Shit. What have I missed?

"It's your turn to introduce yourself," Gina whispers in my ear.

I nod and clear my throat while my brain digs into the lines I was practicing during my shower and my trip to work. Taking a deep breath, I force myself to make eye contact with everyone in the room, except Mr. Knight whose eyes are boring into mine now.

"Good morning, everyone. I'm Charlotte Garnett, but you can call me Charlie or Char; I will respond to either of them." I flash them a smile which I hope doesn't come off as a nervous wince. "My educational background is in business management, and I spent my last five years working in the construction industry. I was an executive assistant for a couple of years to start with, then I began my career in marketing and sales from there. And now, here I am. It's an honor to be given this opportunity and be a part of your respectful team. Your support and guidance will be very much appreciated."

My introduction ends with applause from my new colleagues, forcing me to push my earlier internal debate to the back of my mind.

My first day goes by faster than expected. It's another introduction day, but more details about my day-to-day job. Sebastian is appointed to be my mentor for my first two months, which means he will introduce me to our clients and show me how things work. Once I get the gist of my work demand, I will be left alone and deal with my own accounts, milking them dry and bringing in as much revenue as possible for this company. Then comes the moment of truth: I will stay or I will need to start looking for a new job.

"Guys, I have a dinner meeting tonight, so I'd like to be home on time," Max announces. I learned from Shanti that he and his wife are counting the days until their third child's arrival. It's his main reason to cut down his usual excessive working hours.

"Me too, today's been crazy," Shanti says as she stands up while tidying up the papers and stationery that have been scattered over her desk. "I'll come early tomorrow to make it up."

"I'm going too," Donna adds, glancing at Sebastian and me. "Sorry guys, you need to get the rest of the data yourself. I'll leave my computer on."

"How far are you with the report?" Max asks, putting on his leather jacket.

Sebastian, who has been burying his face in the computer screen, leans back against his seat headrest and runs his fingers through his blond hair. "Almost done. Fifteen minutes tops, then we're off. Gina is not coming back from the meeting, is she?"

"Not that I know. This client is very stiff and bureaucratic. They're giving her a real headache this time. Such a beadle-dom." Max shakes his head. "Alright, I'm off."

Once Max and the girls disappear behind the office door, Sebastian and I resume working on the report. This is a part of the training where I can learn about last month's figures and what to expect this month. I wish I could join the girls and call it a day because I'm tired. People say the first day at work is always draining, and I can confirm that.

I glance at the time on the computer screen that reads 5:29 PM. Chloe is with my sister right now, probably getting ready to be picked up soon. I need to call Sophie as soon as the report is done to let her know that I'm going to be late today.

"Do you have a date or something? You keep staring at the time," Sebastian asks.

"Oh no. I was thinking about my daughter and what to eat for dinner," I reply, laughing at how far my mind has drifted off from work.

Sebastian raises his eyebrows. "You have a daughter, too? Sweet! How old is she?"

"Seven. Well, she is turning eight this summer. How old is yours?"

Sebastian knits his eyebrows. "Oh wow! Almost eight already! Ours just turned three last month." He pauses, seeming hesitant about what he's going to say. "Not trying to be nosey, but you're barely thirty. You had her pretty young, huh?"

"Yeah."

I see the curious glint in his eyes but I decide not to give him further information about my situation with Chloe. This is a topic I prefer to keep private because I've chosen to lie to my own daughter. I'm not planning to turn it into a public deception.

Chloe started to ask about who her father was and his whereabouts when she was three. I couldn't answer her with "you were conceived during a drunken night and I don't know who your papa is". So, I lied. A white lie, of course. I told her that her father was Ethan, my college sweetheart, but sadly we didn't work out. We'd broken up before we found out I was pregnant with her, and Ethan had moved to the other side of the globe. We have lost contact ever since. I know I have to tell her the truth one day, but the day just hasn't come yet. I just can't bring myself to tell her that she was made during a one-night stand unintentionally because of the stupid broken condom.

The sound of chair wheels gliding across the floor pulls me out of my thoughts. Sebastian gets up and walks to the printer. After collecting the papers, he puts them on my desk. "If you can bring this upstairs, I will get the stuff for tomorrow's client meeting ready. Then we can leave this building before six."

"Upstairs?"

"To Mr. Knight's desk. He's expecting this today."

My heart leaps when I hear his name. "Can I just leave this on his secretary's desk?"

"Sure if someone is sitting there, but his assistant resigned, remember? Hmm, maybe he got an emergency replacement for today. You will find out soon enough." Sebastian shrugs as he plops down on his seat and starts rummaging through his shelf.

"Okay." I get up and grab the document. "Umm, thirteenth floor, right?"

"The one and only. The very lucky number for the badasses."

The trip to the thirteenth floor is torture. The thought of meeting Mr. Knight again gives me a twist in the stomach, and I can't even blame anyone for this.

After the kick-off meeting ended this morning, he came to me and shook my hand, welcoming me to Knight & Co. He was friendly yet distant, and there was no sign that he recognized me. Weirdly, it gave me a mixed feeling of relief and...disappointment?

Despite my attempt to ignore the tingling suspicion about him being Chloe's biological father, the thought keeps bugging me all day. And I don't know how to stop this.

Once the elevator doors slide open, I'm met with an office directory board where I can find my CEO's room. The thirteenth level is exclusively reserved for the directors of Remington Group and the chiefs of its subsidiaries. Unlike the layout on the fourth floor, all rooms here are separated by a normal wall. What a luxury of being on the top of the organization charts. Their privacy is well prioritized while we, who sit at the bottom of the chart, are blessed by a half-height partition. Hails, cubicles!

I groan when I see no one behind Mr. Knight's assistant's desk. Great. What do I do now? Knock on his door? Slide the papers through the gap under his door? Or run back to the fourth floor? Well, the idea of bolting out is tempting but I'd rather get my job done on my first working day.

Standing in front of his door, my eyes are glued to the nameplate on his door: Ashton Knight.

"Come in!" a deep voice echoes from inside the room. Is he in the middle of talking with someone now? Should I go back later?

"The door isn't locked! Just go in!"

Huh? Is it directed to me? But he can't see me standing behind his door, can he? And he definitely can't see me through the wall, unless he's Superman with an X-ray vision.

Not feeling convinced, I look around, wondering if maybe the voice is coming from somewhere else. But there is no one in sight. Before I know it, the door in front of me swings open, revealing the man I dread seeing.

Mr. Knight doesn't look pleased at all. He scowls at me as his hand extends to demand the papers in my hand impatiently.

"Ms. Garnett, try to be more efficient next time. I hate repeating myself."

I stare at him dumbfounded. He did talk to me. "I-I am sorry. I thought I heard a voice but I wasn't sure."

He raises his eyebrows. "You weren't sure you heard a voice?"

"I mean I heard a voice but I wasn't sure if it was you talking to me."

"Do you have issues with hallucinations, Ms. Garnett?"

"Excuse me?"

"Hallucinations. Hearing things in your head."

I frown, feeling offended all of a sudden. This man and his nasty mouth. "No, I don't. I was just" -I look around again- "curious. How did you know I was standing here?"

Mr. Knight gives me a disturbingly stoic look. "Have you checked what is sitting above your head?"

I look up and inwardly scold myself. Of course, there is a camera. "Oh."

"Nice observation skills. I wonder how you will manage to get through your six months," he says. "And I need coffee. Black, no sugar. Can you get that? Thank you." With that, he takes the document from my hand and heads back to his desk.

Chapter 5

I need coffee. Black, no sugar. Thank you.

His buffalo voice keeps replaying in my head. Who the hell does he think he is? Fine, he's the boss of my boss, which means he's my boss too, but still, he has no right to be disrespectful to me or to treat me like shit. Maybe I should show him real shit.

After rummaging through the pantry cupboard, I pull out a white cup with the Remington logo on it since I have no idea which one is his. Not that I give a damn. I could have just grabbed the dirty one from the sink if there was none left in the cupboard for all I care. It's true that I used to be an executive assistant several years back, and sometimes, my ex-boss asked me nicely to make him coffee when the tea ladies had left work, and I did it gladly because I didn't see it as an issue. My only problem now is his face.

Despite the organizational hierarchy, everyone should treat each other with respect. A toxic work environment is a big red flag, to begin with. Maybe behind the big name of the Remington Group, this job isn't worth it after all.

While waiting for the coffee machine to brew, I fish my phone out of my pocket and dial my sister's number. "Hey, Soph," I greet with a relieved sigh after hearing a familiar voice from the other side. "I'm going to be late tonight. I don't think I will make it there before dinner."

"Don't worry about it. You guys can always eat dinner with us. Chloe is in Diana's room now, having girl time, and I'm not allowed to join them." Sophie chuckles.

"At least some of us are having fun."

"Yeah." I hear a shuffling sound in the background. Knowing her, she must be preparing dinner right now. "How's work?"

"The work is fine. Still need to learn more before they let me handle my own accounts."

"Okay...but do I hear a 'but' here?"

I put my hand behind my neck and massage it softly. "My big boss is a capital A." Realizing that someone might hear me, I scoot to the pantry door and stick my head out to check the hallway. Luckily, it's as dead as when I came in. "I have to stay back because I'm making his damn coffee right now."

"Huh? Did you apply for the wrong position?"

"Of course not. I'll tell you the whole story later. I need to plan for revenge now then I'll be on my way to your place."

"Char, what are you going to do?" she asks, her tone reminding me of the day I decided to move out with Chloe from our parents' house.

I shrug and tell her the truth. "I don't know yet."

"Don't do anything stupid. People would kill to be in your position now."

And they will be literally killed after they get in. "Yeah okay. No one will get killed tonight, don't worry," I reply in a dismissive tone.

"Why am I not convinced?"

"The coffee is almost ready. I'll see you in an hour or so. Bye," I hang up before my sister can mutter any more words.

I slip my phone back into my pocket and chuckle softly, thinking about how different Sophie and I are. She has always been the considerate and sensible big sister, while I'm the impulsive and immature one. I remember how our parents used to compare us and wished I would've been more like her to spare them a headache. But hey, who can choose their personality? I'm just glad that they finally see that I'm not Sophie, and that they know damn well how hard I've tried to be what they want.

The coffee machine spits a gurgling sound, pulling me back to my current state of mind. Coffee. Black. No sugar. Asshole.

Waiting for the noise to stop completely, my eyes roam over the pantry shelves, casually scanning what the tea ladies store for the executive floor. Salt, sugar, pepper, ketchup, mustard– My eyes stumble upon the small bottle with red liquid in it.

Nice observation skills.

Damn right.

I'm knocking on his door this time. Once his voice tells me to enter his room, I open the door and walk in with the most stunning smile I can muster.

His room is huge and neat. The wall is painted dark blue with a large window displaying the city view. A yellow sofa, a coffee table, and a blue reading chair are situated on one side of the room, and a big mahogany desk on the other side. A gigantic bookshelf stands intimidatingly against the wall behind his managerial desk. Mr. Knight stands up when he sees me walking in his direction. He slips his hands into his pockets, plops down on the corner of his table, and crosses his leg over the other while his eyes are on me.

I keep my cool as I prepare myself for another round of insults he is probably going to throw at my face. "Your coffee, sir." I put the cup carefully on his desk, next to his other empty cup. I'm just hoping he doesn't catch my slightly trembling hand; the hand that is convicted of a misdeed.

"Ms. Garnett," he says gently.

"Sir?"

He sighs. "I was being too harsh earlier. That was not very professional of me. I apologize for that."

I stand rooted to my spot, not believing my ears. Did he just...?

"And I didn't mean to insult your skills. Max and I were through your profile and agreed that you have the qualities that we're looking for," he adds. "I hope what happened today doesn't give you the wrong idea. You know that things can be stressful and put a lot of strain on us, but most of the time, we are a solid team and we support each other."

I shift my gaze to him and am met with a pair of emerald green irises that are staring back at me. From the glints in his eyes, he seems to be sincerely remorseful but at the same time, his civil yet guarded attitude is back, exactly the same Mr. Knight I saw in the meeting room this morning.

"That's fine. I understand that perfectly, Mr. Knight," I reply, forcing a smile at him. "And I'm looking forward to contributing to our team."

Mr. Knight smiles back at me, making my traitorous heart leap. He then nods and props himself up. "Excellent. I'll see you tomorrow then." With that, he turns on his heels and heads back to his chair.

That is my cue to leave but my feet are glued to the floor as a realization dawns on me. I emptied one-third of the ghost chili sauce into his coffee because I wanted him to pay for the nasty attitude he gave me earlier. I was so pissed at him that I didn't think further about the consequences. I didn't care if I would get fired or if I had to find another job tomorrow because in my five years of working experience, I've never been treated like trash. My former boss wasn't an easy man, but he treated his subordinates kindly, and that was the reason I stayed in his company for so long without a clear career path.

Learning about what kind of person my current CEO is, I don't hold my breath about having long-term employment here. Still, what I'm doing now is a little bit too far and immature. He is my big boss for god sake. Despite his overbearing attitude and sharp words, he has the guts to apologize to his staff, which I truly appreciate, and it makes me feel even guiltier for spicing up his coffee.

What do I do now?

My breath hitches in my throat when his hand stretches out to reach for the deadly cup on his desk. Out of reflex, I grab the other side of its saucer, preventing it from moving closer to him. He frowns and pulls the saucer harder but my fingers clutch the other side of it for dear life.

"Ms. Garnett."

"Yes, sir?"

"I think you're grabbing the wrong cup," he says. "This is not the empty one."

"Oh. My bad." Yet I refuse to let it go.

Annoyance begins to sneak on his face. He knits his eyebrows before his full glare is directed at me. "What–"

"Am I interrupting something?" A feminine voice from behind me prompts us to stop the pulling competition and turn our heads to the source of the distraction.

A gorgeous woman in a red dress is standing at the doorway. Her wavy blonde hair cascades over her shoulders, glowing under the sconce of golden light that is hanging next to the door frame. She wears red lipstick, contrasting her pale complexion and she looks dazzling. The only thing that's missing is a fan to blow her hair as she's making her entrance.

I can feel Mr. Knight's grip loosen on the saucer. "What are you doing here?" he asks in his buffalo voice, almost growling.

The woman raises her eyebrows as she saunters in our direction. "Is that how you greet your sister after months of not making time to see her? Where have all your manners gone, my little brother?" The woman turns her head to me.

"And she must be your new assistant. I didn't know you'd changed your mind about having a female assistant."

"It's none of your goddamn business," Mr. Knight says curtly before shifting his gaze to me. "You may leave, Ms. Garnett."

"Yes, sir," I answer while attempting to take the cup with me once again.

"Ms. Garnett! Leave my cup on the table, please." If a glare could kill, I would be six feet under right now.

"Oh, yeah, sorry." I grab his empty cup instead and trudge to the door, defeated.

It's happening again. My impulsiveness has taken over my rational mind and now I have to deal with the consequences that I'm going to regret. I do need to start calling around tomorrow and send my resume to all the job openings I can find on the internet.

After placing the empty cup into the sink, I make my way to the elevator, with my head down and shoulders slumping. Had I never touched that criminal sauce and just swallowed my pride, things would have been so much different. All I can do now is hope that he doesn't taste the spiciness in his coffee, which is highly unlikely. He will notice it right away, and tomorrow will be my last day working for this company.

I wonder if he will spurt the coffee out of his mouth once he sips it or if he will just gulp it before the burning sensation starts to smolder his throat. Wait, what if he is spicy food intolerant?

Shit! What have I done?

The elevator doors slide open but I pivot on my heels and run back to Mr. Knight's room. I have to get that cup back for whatever reason. I will risk getting fired right here right now than living with the guilt of murdering my boss.

As I come closer to his room, I hear a heated argument between the two siblings. Mr. Knight's sister is half yelling in her high-pitched voice, matching her brother's guttural voice. They sound almost like a baboon and a buffalo dueting in a serene jungle. I stop at the doorway, thinking about what I'm going to do next when Mr. Knight's sister grabs the cup on his desk and throws the contents at her brother's face.

Chapter 6

"Do I have to?" Chloe whines once I bring up the topic of the school shuttle bus. She doesn't like the idea of it for some reason. Maybe because I have always brought her to school myself since day one.

We, again, are now stuck at the intersection, waiting for our turn to get out of this horrendous traffic. If I said earlier I hated Monday, now I'm starting to believe that Tuesday is no better.

"Yeah, I've been thinking about this. I'm planning to take a train to work instead of driving there."

Chloe takes a deep breath and sighs loudly. Such a drama queen she is. "Does it mean I have to get up earlier?"

"Yeah."

She moans and grunts at my reply as if the world has turned against her completely.

Chloe hates waking up in the morning. She used to be an early bird, but since last year, she's developed a new unhealthy attachment to her bed. Waking her up is becoming a new chore for me. Well, she is my kid after all. I still remember how my mom used to prank me to get me out of my bed.

"If I have to drop you off first, we still have to start earlier anyway, so that I can catch the train on time." I'm eyeing her from the rear-view mirror. "It doesn't matter if I take you to school or if you go by bus, you will need to wake up earlier, sweetie. And the train station is closer to our home, it's just more practical for you to go with the shuttle bus."

"What if the kids on the same bus are mean? Marissa gets annoyed a lot by the boys on the same bus with her."

"Have those kids done something to Marissa?"

"Well, they often bother her, like hiding her stuff or pulling her hair."

I frown. "Hmm, has Marissa told her parents about this? Or maybe told the bus dispatcher?"

Chloe shrugs. "I don't know."

"She should. Tell her to."

"Okay."

"And don't worry, I'm going to make sure you get the best shuttle bus with maximum control." I hit the accelerator once the traffic light turns green. "But if other kids in the same bus try to bully you, you know what to do. Remember last summer when you fought the boy in your class? This is no different. But then you need to tell me right away."

"But the headmaster said fighting is not good."

I bite my lower lip, thinking about what to answer her. "True. If you can avoid it, then it's better to stay clear of it. But if a boy hits you like last time, I permit you to hit him back. A boy should never hit a girl." I glance at my daughter who is listening to me religiously. I add, "We should never hit anyone. But if they attack us first, then it's okay to defend ourselves by attacking back. Do you understand?"

Chloe nods. "Yes."

My daughter's school finally comes into view. I slowly pull over several meters before the gate. When the car stops fully, I turn my head to watch her getting out of her seat booster. "We'll talk more about this tonight, okay?"

"Are you going to be at aunt Sophie's on time tonight?"

"Yes, I hope so."

"'Kay. See you tonight, Mama." She leans over to give me a peck before jumping out of the car.

"Enjoy school!"

Smiling, I watch her zigzagging toward her school gate. Her long brown hair dances in the air as the wind gusts through. Her small torso is hidden behind her polka-dot red backpack, making her look like a walking ladybug.

Chloe was born lightweight. I remember how I blamed myself for that since I believed it was because of my alcohol consumption in my first trimester of pregnancy. Even though it wasn't intentional and the doctor didn't confirm it, the guilt refused to leave me for a very long time. I'm just glad that she is starting to catch up with the average size of kids her age now.

Chloe turns her head as she grins and waves at me before disappearing behind her school iron gate. An instant rush of warmth blankets my heart. That little girl has no idea what she's doing to her mother.

It's the second day of work, and I hope my lucky stars are still beaming somewhere up above. Yesterday evening, I was darn sure I would lose my job, but here I am now, ready to tackle my next challenge at work.

I take a deep breath and stride confidently to my cubicle.

"Good morning, Charlie!" Sebastian greets me, a little too enthusiastic, but it's not enough to hide the odd glint in his eyes when he looks at me.

I picked a classier work attire today. A royal blue dress with a square neckline and beige pumps -something I never did at my previous work. I always received compliments every time I wore this dress and that is the very reason I'm wearing it today, to cast away bad luck during my first day of meeting clients. But I'm not sure if Sebastian's gaze is referring to my dazzling appearance right now. My gut feeling says it's something else but I push it aside. A guilty person tends to get paranoid, right?

"Morning," I reply while looking at the empty cubicles next to mine. "Where are the girls?"

"At the pantry. They often have their breakfast together before work," Sebastian answers before glancing at his wrist-watch. "They should be here soon."

"Okay." I put my bag on my seat before leaning against my desk, almost sitting on it. "So, what time are we leaving for the first client's meeting? I can drive if you like."

Sebastian taps her pen against his desk. "About that... I think Max wants to have a word with you first." With that, his gaze shifts to Max's glass door behind me, making my bright smile freeze and my breath stuck in my throat. "It sounds urgent."

Urgent doesn't sound good. Does it have anything to do with the incident yesterday evening? Am I in trouble? Am I getting fired? "No!" I squeak but quickly correct myself, "I mean, no problem. Sure. Is he inside now?"

"Yeah, he's been waiting for you."

I nod and stand up, calmly adjusting my dress while feeling like a wrecking ball inside. This is it. I'm finished. My career at this multi-billionaire company ends as fast as it starts, drowning in a pool of black coffee with ghost chili sauce in it.

Yesterday was a total mess. After Emily Knight threw the spiced coffee at her brother's face, she stormed out and never looked back, leaving me alone with my drenched CEO. Seeing his expression at that very moment, I would have laughed if my job wasn't in jeopardy. So, I grabbed a box of tissue from the coffee table and rushed to him.

The next scene was a blur. I helped him dry up, I grabbed a towel soaked in milk to dab on his face and neck to prevent it from burning, and I sprinted to his car in the basement to grab his extra clothes. He complained about the unusual prickling sensation on his skin, but I assured him that was just the irritation from the boiling-hot coffee. Nothing more nothing less.

Following my suggestion, Mr. Knight washed his face in the restroom while I wiped his desk and took the cup back to the pantry, clearing the crime scene. I was just hoping that he hadn't tasted the spiciness on his lips since Emily threw it straight at his face and neck area.

He came back to his room with his reddish face and a clean shirt. When he said nothing about the suspicious spiciness, I sighed in relief. Still, I went home wondering if he actually knew something was off and finally put two and two together.

Apparently, he did. Otherwise, I won't be here, standing in front of Max's door that is already open.

I knock softly. "Good morning, Max. Sebastian said you wanted to talk to me."

Max, who is bending over and rummaging through his drawers, turns his head to me and smiles. "Good Morning, Charlotte. Yes. Please come in. Close the door behind you, will you?"

"Okay." I close the door and walk to his desk. I've never been fired before, but I know it's going to be as sucky as when my ex broke up with me. I sit down and wait until he's done fishing some files out of the drawer.

"So," he says after throwing the documents to his desk, "we have a situation right now."

I gulp the imaginary lump in my throat. "Okay."

"It's about our big boss, Mr. Knight," he adds.

Panic courses my entire body. "I can explain," I squeak.

Max frowns. "Huh?"

Noticing the confused look on his face, I inwardly scold myself. Obviously, we aren't on the same page. Maybe I'm not being fired. "I mean, can you explain further... please?"

The frown hasn't left his face but he nods. "Mr. Knight's executive assistant resigned yesterday without notice, and the HR department is trying to find his replacement as soon as possible. In the meantime, he needs someone to help him with phone calls and schedules."

I'm holding my breath. I don't like where this is going.

"And since you have the experience of being a secretary to a president director, and considering that you haven't started with your accounts, he wants you to take the executive assistant position temporarily."

"Oh."

"It's just for a week." Max winces, and I know right away he's lying about the time frame.

I clear my throat. "Thanks for the offer. But I don't think it's a good idea, Max. You see, I only have six months to prove myself to this team. If I go to the thirteenth floor and start this job later, how will I achieve my target in time?" I try to wriggle my way out of it.

"This isn't an offer, Charlotte," Max replies softly.

"What?"

"Mr. Knight assigns you to fill the temporary position."

I can't believe my ears. "He can't make me. This is against the contract we signed!"

Max knits his eyebrows. "Oh? He said you would do this after the conversation you two had yesterday."

"Huh? What conversation?"

"The one over a company you're planning to tap since the CEO happens to be his old friend. He said you would help him out with the secretary task if he agreed to help you connect with the man. I honestly think this is a good opportunity for you, Charlotte."

I'm trying to recall every scene on the thirteenth floor yesterday but nothing about approaching a new company comes up. Am I having partial amnesia? Or is Mr. Knight having hallucinations? I'm beyond confused. "Are you sure he was talking about me?"

"Of course. There's only one Charlotte Garnett in this office."

Something is definitely wrong. It doesn't feel good. "And what company was he talking about if I may ask?"

"I'm not sure he mentioned the company name, but it's the one that produces your favorite brand of ghost chili sauce. Rompa Rampa, is it?"

I'm almost tipping off the seat. My heart drums wildly against my chest and my stomach churns. He knows. He noticed it. I fucking knew it.

Is this my punishment for my attempt to prank him? What if I refuse? Will he fire me on the spot? Or worse, will he sue me? But he has no proof, right? I got rid of all the evidence.

My breath hitches in my throat. The camera surveillance.

"Is there a camera in the pantry room on the thirteenth floor?" I ask in horror.

Max seems surprised by my random question. "Uh, I believe so. The thirteenth floor has cameras almost in every corner of it. Why do you ask?"

I feel my vigor leaving my body once I realize I'm being blackmailed by my own boss. What is his plan? Is he going to enslave me from 6 A.M to 9 P.M every single day? Is he going to poison my drink for revenge? Oh shit, am I going to die alone and unheard on the empty and eerie thirteenth floor?

"Charlotte? Charlie?" The next thing I know, Max is waving his hand in front of my face. "Are you alright?"

"Y-yes... I'm fine," I answer after I can find my voice. "When do I start?"

"As soon as you're ready."

"Does it mean today?"

"It means now."

Chapter 7

Walking with my tail between my legs, I pray that the person I dread seeing is not sitting in his room. Max told me that Mr. Knight was leaving for an event this morning, and he would appreciate it if I could start with the assistant role before his departure. And I, of course, stalled as long as I could until I had no more reason to postpone my trip to the thirteenth level.

Surprisingly, the executive floor isn't as dead as yesterday evening. Every secretarial desk situated in front of its executive's room has a human sitting behind it, except for the one for my CEO. The hum of people conversing, telephones beeping, and the sound of fingers dancing furiously on the keyboard fill the air. The door of the room between the elevator and Mr. Knight's is now open, revealing a huge desk with Mr. Tan sitting on it, frowning while reading a paper in his hand. I jump as laughter booms, followed by two men in their forties emerging from the room at the end of the hallway. Where were these people yesterday?

I trudge to Mr. Knight's door which to my dismay, is slightly open; a sign that he is still here. Dammit! My eyes roam over the empty executive assistant desk that stands proudly as if it's staring back at me mockingly. It's an L-shaped table with two computer screens sitting on it. A half-length cabinet is placed against the wall, behind the assistant chair, adorned by decorative floating shelves hanging above it. This working space looks more luxurious than the one we have downstairs despite the fact that we are the ones who bring the revenue to this company. How convenient!

"You're here. Good."

I have no idea how long Mr. Knight has been standing at his doorway. His handsome face isn't as red as when I left yesterday, but I still can see the flush around his nose and mouth. His sharp gaze is fixed on me, making my already corrupted courage shrink even more. I whimper inwardly.

Should I apologize? But doesn't it mean I admit defeat? Because despite my regret for succumbing to my impulsiveness, I don't feel guilty. He deserved it. But will he make my life a living hell if I don't apologize? Maybe I should then.

"Mr. Knight, I apologize..." I start my line but my tongue betrays me, "for not being able to arrive here sooner."

Mr. Knight raises his eyebrows slightly, but his face remains stoic. "I believe Max explained the predicament we have at the moment. Thus, this isn't permanent, and take this as an opportunity to learn."

The way he stresses the words 'predicament' and 'learn' makes me shiver. Why does he sound so ominous? Does he mean we as a company or we as Charlotte Garnett and

Ashton Knight? He doesn't know that I know the part about the chili sauce producer bullshit, right? He wasn't there when Max told me about it. So, let's just pretend that Max never brought that up. Let's settle with me taking the assignment without any questions because I'm a good employee.

"Yes, sir."

"For this morning, I won't ask much from you except to clear all the schedules I have today after four. If I have an appointment with a client, cancel it and make a new one. Summon every dept head for an urgent meeting this afternoon, anywhere between four and six is good."

I hurry to the desk and yank post-it notes and a pen next to the computer screen. Quickly, I jot down his instructions.

"I will be out for an event and I won't be back before lunch, but when I'm back, I want my coffee on my desk. Please, do not trouble yourself by making it this time." He takes his wallet out of his pocket and pulls out a blue card before tossing it to my table. "I want you to go to the coffee shop in the building across the street. And I want it black. Any questions?"

I gulp, feeling my throat dry instantly. "No, sir."

"Good. You can study this week's schedules that Alex had set before he left and prepare the documents accordingly. And, Ms. Garnett, I don't want any disturbance. Any call or inquiry that has nothing to do with this company shall be rejected."

"Duly noted, sir."

"Excellent. Welcome to the thirteenth floor and I'm sure you will gain an unforgettable experience here."

I glance at the time on my phone and sigh. It feels like it was just five minutes ago when I joined the girls in the cafeteria for lunch, and now it's time to continue my life as a temporary secretary to my CEO. I collect all my trash and pile it on my tray.

Gina frowns. "You need to go back already? Does he not let you have your full lunch break?"

I shake my head. "No, it's not that. I need to grab his coffee from across the street before I go up. I'm just not sure how busy the coffee shop is."

"It's busy all the time and getting him his coffee is not your job," Gina retorts.

"Yeah. Alex never picked up his coffee from the shop, either," Donna chips in. "Is John not coming today then?"

"John?" I ask.

"Yeah, the errand boy for the executive floor," Donna replies.

"Uh, there was a guy who took some documents from the other secretary's desks to distribute them to the entire building, but I'm not sure if he was John," I mumble. "Anyway, it doesn't matter for now. I'm done eating anyway. I can also grab a hot cappuccino for myself." I shrug as I make a mental note to find out about how this beverage stuff works.

After saying goodbye to the girls, I make my way out of the cafeteria and straight to exit the Remington building. While waltzing through the cold wind to the skyscraper across the street, I can't help pondering how surreal my day has been. How did I end up being in this situation? How did I start a war with my boss?

After three years of building my skills and qualifications in sales and marketing, I don't want to go back to the secretary job again. I don't want to be stuck behind the desk, making schedules for my boss, or talking on the phone to whoever is on the other side of the line. I like to meet and connect with other professionals. I love to define who and what my targets are and my adrenaline rushes for the challenge to pursue them.

I sigh again. This, too, shall pass. It's just temporary. Play it smart, Char.

Suits 'N Beans is beyond busy. Apparently, it's the only coffee shop on this business street and is situated on the ground floor of the most prestigious office building in the city. I'm in awe when I enter the shop. It's like a campfire in the middle of a snowfield. The rustic design contrasts the cold and modern ambiance of the rest of the building.

Just as Gina said, all tables in the shop are occupied and people are standing in a rather long queue by the counter. I bet, in the chill February weather like now, hot beverages and some pastries are in high demand. Begrudgingly, I position myself at the tail of the line. I'm just hoping I'll make it on time when I'm back.

I'm on my phone, checking my social media, when someone bumps into me, followed by a baritone voice apologizing.

"I'm sorry, miss, I wasn't..." the man's voice falters once I crane my neck to look up, "Char?"

I feel the world stop spinning. The phone in my hand almost slips through my finger, but I quickly tighten my grip on it. It takes me several seconds before I can respond. "Ethan."

"What are you doing here?" Ethan asks in disbelief. He rubs his face before running his fingers through his jet-black hair; just exactly how I remember it every time he's caught by surprise.

"I can ask the same question!" I answer while forcing myself to smile.

"I'm working here, I mean in this building, up there," he points a finger at the ceiling, "in a law firm. What about you?"

"I just started working for the Remington group. It's my second week."

"Oh, wow, cool. I heard it's quite a challenge to get a spot there. Congratulations, Char!"

"Thank you." I grin, not sure what to say next; my brain suddenly bails on me. I thought my day couldn't go any weirder than it already was, but here I am, running into my ex who I believed was already swallowed by a hippo or something. He is also the ex that still becomes a part of my life now. Well, without his consent, of course.

I stopped dreaming about getting back with Ethan once Chloe was born. He did reach out to me a few months after the breakup, confessing that as much as he was hurt, he couldn't get over me. It was the same week when I found out I was pregnant with Chloe. The timing was just not in our favor. In the next six months, he was transferred to another university across the country, and I've never heard from him ever since.

"Hey Char, I do need to get going now, but I'd like to catch up sometime if you're up for it." Ethan hands his coffee to the younger guy in a suit who has been standing next to him, quietly eyeing our encounter. He pulls his wallet out of his pocket before taking a silver name card. "Call me or text me. Maybe we can meet up for lunch sometime this week or next week?"

I take his card and read it briefly. Ethan Watkins, a senior associate. "Sure. I haven't had a business card to exchange yet, but I'll give you a call."

"I'm looking forward to it." He flashes me a smile that haunted my dream for years.

"Seems like you're happy with your new job," Mr. Knight says when he sees me walk to his desk with his black coffee in my hand.

"A temporary job," I correct him. "And why is that, sir?"

"You wouldn't be smiling brightly if you disliked this role, would you?"

"Oh. Yeah, of course," I reply, placing his coffee and his corporate credit card on his desk. I don't need to tell him the real reason why I've been grinning like a giddy schoolgirl since I left the coffee shop. "This is very generous of you to give me this valuable opportunity."

"And you're late."

"Lunchtime finishes at one and it's two minutes to one o'clock. I'm not late."

"I said I want my coffee ready when I'm back, not when the lunch break is over."

I curl my finger into a fist. Don't fall into this trap, don't fall into this trap, do not fall. "My apologies. I will pay better attention to your instructions next time."

"You better." He nods as he picks up his cup and brings it to his lip. Carefully, he takes a small sip from it and pauses, probably to make sure if it wasn't spiced or something, before taking another sip. A bigger one. "I want the documents for today's meeting printed out. Everyone needs to have a copy."

"Sure. Anything else, sir?"

"You can take the card with you, because I will need you to get my beverage or maybe a snack from the store, regularly. That's all for now."

"Yes, sir." I take the card back before turning on my heels and striding to the door.

"One more thing," Mr. Knight's voice stops me. "Have we, by any chance... met before?"

My heart leaps as I stand rooted on my spot. Oh, no. I slowly turn myself to him, giving him the best smile I can muster. "I'm not sure. Have we?"

"I asked you first, Charlotte." He leans back against his seat, sipping his coffee while his eyes are boring into mine. "Never mind. Maybe I've mistaken you for someone else."

"That's possible, sir. Highly possible," I answer, a little bit too quickly. "I'm going to... get the document ready."

As Mr. Knight nods, I walk, scratch that, I dash out of his room and close the door behind me. What does he remember? Is it something involving a wild frat party eight years ago? Does it mean he really is Chloe's father? I've been pushing the thought to the back of my mind because deep down, I'm not ready to deal with this. Not yet.

All of a sudden, I can't feel my legs properly but I fight the urge to lean against his door. He still can see me from the damn camera. Trying to compose myself, I trudge to my seat and begin collecting all the files I need to print out. Yet, my mind keeps jumping back to the conversation I had just now with my boss. It's when the elevator makes a ding sound, revealing the boy I saw this morning, carrying a tray full of coffee cups with the 'Suits 'n Beans' logo.

He stops at Mr. Tan's secretary's desk and hands the paper tray to the assistant. "Two cappuccinos, three long-blacks, and one latte."

"Thank you, John. I can't imagine my life without you!" Tanya, Mr. Tan's secretary, says in a sing-song.

"Oh I can, that would be horrendous," says the boy, grinning. As if he notices that he's being stared at, he turns his head to me. "Hullo, miss... You must be Mr. Knight's new assistant. I'm John, the thirteenth-floor hero. Anything related to document distribution or picking up something from outside this building, I will be at your service."

"Hello, John. I'm Charlotte. A pleasure to meet you." I get out of my desk and walk to him so that I don't need to talk loudly, to make sure the initial person doesn't hear our conversation. "Actually, I have a question."

"And what would that be?"

"Do you also take care of Mr. Knight's beverage?"

"Always," he replies proudly. "I mean, only when he's around. But he told me he didn't need my service today. So, I guess he's not in his office now?"

I can hear myself growling. "No, he's inside," I answer while gritting my teeth. "Thank you, John. I might need your service a lot in the next few days."

"Aye, aye, miss!"

Chapter 8

When Mr. Knight said I would get an unforgettable experience working on the executive floor, he meant it.

The real shit began the next day. Meeting after meeting, never-ending phone calls and email correspondence, problems with the departments that didn't follow through with the deadlines, issues with vendors who provided meals and beverages for the meetings, and the list kept adding up. It was like a Deja Vu. Only, it was worse.

After our last encounter, Mr. Knight and I haven't had a chance to have another social chat. He was either burying his face in his computer screen, grunting and growling at someone on the phone, or stuck in back-to-back appointments. When I wasn't in the meeting room to take minutes, we communicated through phone or email. And that was good because his presence was still too intimidating for me; hell, it's still menacing now.

On top of that, something inside my head keeps reminding me that I'm not yet off the hook. He knows about the ghost chili incident, but he hasn't used it against me. The suspense is killing me. I should have apologized in the first place.

Days go by faster than the speed of light, and now I've been doing the executive assistant job for almost two weeks. Did Max mention the temporary position was only for a week? A week my ass.

Mr. Knight interviewed five candidates who had been through Human Resource screening, but none of them gets hired. Only heaven knows the reason. He simply doesn't want to pull down the bar a little bit and give the best candidate a shot. Maybe he forgets that there is a support system called training where employees can upgrade their skills. Also, I still don't get why he doesn't want to have a female assistant. It would have made the Human Resources job ten times easier to find Alex's replacement.

The waiting makes me anxious because I don't know how much longer I can keep up with this temporary task. This isn't the job for me. I should have been on the fourth floor by now.

"You know, I'm surprised that Mr. Knight chose a female temporary assistant," chirps Tanya who is now having breakfast with me in the pantry. We rarely do this because of the workload that sometimes leaves us no choice but to eat at our table.

I raise my eyebrow while scooping my almost-empty blueberry yogurt with a spoon. "How so? Is he a gynophobia?"

"What phobia?"

"Fear of women."

"Oh!" Tanya laughs at my reply. "No! hell, no."

I chug down the rest of my yogurt by tipping the cup over my mouth. "Then why doesn't he want to have a female assistant?"

"Um, not sure." Tanya bites her lower lip while her eyes twinkle; the look a girl has when she's so close to spilling juicy gossip.

"Too bad. I've been so curious about it." I purse my lips while counting inwardly.

One... two... three.

"Rumor has it that he got involved with a female secretary who happened to be an assistant of the previous CEO, Mr. D. Knight. Things got messy because apparently, this girl was also seeing her CEO secretly. At. The. Same. Time! Then the war began. There was even an office fight between the two because of the girl. But," Tanya shrugs, contrasting her enthusiasm in cooking up the story, "we never know what actually happened. No one really witnessed the fight."

"Wait, Mr. D. Knight is Mr. Ashton Knight's father?"

"No." Tanya shakes her head. "He is the big brother, Dickson Knight. As you see, Knight Corporation used to be a family business until it went public seven years ago. So, when this company joined the Remington group, Mr. D. Knight was the CEO, replacing their sick father. But it didn't go well. He wasn't capable of leading a company with a different level of demands and pressure. One day he messed up, big time, and he was forced to step down."

"Oh."

"But we're glad that he stepped down. He isn't a nice man. True to his name, Dickson, he's a dick."

This is getting juicy. I glance at the clock above the pantry door, indicating that I still have ten minutes more for office gossip. Turning around in my seat, I face her again. "What happened to the girl by the way?"

"Honestly, I don't know. I've never met her because it happened a few years back before I joined this company. I only heard she resigned after the big catastrophe in the office, but Mr. Ashton Knight was still seeing her for a while. Seems like he was so head over heels for her. After a while, the girl was out of the radar, no one knew where she was or what happened to her. Especially after Mr. Knight took over the CEO seat, no one dares to make a speculation about him and the secretary."

"I see." I glance at the camera on the corner of the ceiling. "Is that camera on by the way? Can it record what we're saying now?"

Tanya follows my eyes. "Nah. It can only see us. No sound recorded. Besides, no one checks our activity in the pantry unless the person has some weird kink."

"Tell me about it," I mumble, glancing at the camera surveillance once more time. "So, the current CEO position, is it being handed over to Mr. Ashton Knight?"

Tanya wrinkles her nose. "I don't believe so. Mr. Ashton Knight got this position last year from the boards' and shareholders' votes. I believe they saw his qualities. I mean, look at him, he's smart, strong-driven, good business instinct and he's reflecting the ruthlessness of his late father. Also, he knows about the Knight company from A to Z, more than anyone else here, except Mr. Tan."

"Oh, okay."

"Hang on there, girl. Mr. Knight can be very demanding and insufferable sometimes, but he's a good man."

"True, he's insufferable. You know what, I think both their names are cursed," I look around to make sure that there is no one else in the pantry before leaning forward, continuing with a low tone, "If Mr. D. Knight is a dick, then Mr. A. Knight must be an ass."

Tanya, who is drinking from her bottle, almost spurs the water out of her mouth. She then throws her head backward, cackling. "That's a rhyme! He's such an ass sometimes. But if you know him closely, he can be nice."

"Well, I haven't seen the sweet part of him. Yet." I put my dirty cutlery back in my breakfast box. "And I'm not gonna wait around to witness it. Because I'm going back to the fourth floor soon."

Tanya mimics my gesture, gathering her stuff and bringing them to the sink. "Have they found a replacement?"

"Not yet. But today, several candidates are set for an interview. I have a good feeling about this."

Well, to be truthful, I don't. But a girl can hope, can't she?

After pondering for days, I finally texted Ethan and we agreed to meet for lunch, which is today. He looked genuinely happy when we bumped into each other a couple of weeks ago. Maybe, just maybe, it's time for us to put all the uni drama behind us. We are now adults and should be able to act civilly toward each other. And in all honesty, I'm curious how he ended up in this city.

Suits 'N Beans is packed as always but luckily I can secure a spot for us. Ethan suggested we have a proper lunch at the well-known Mexican restaurant around the corner, but I refused the idea. I haven't seen him for more than eight years and I'm not sure if I want to meet him in an exclusive place like that. A coffee shop feels more casual, lighter, and easy to escape if things go awkward.

Luckily, it doesn't.

The conversation flows easily like two good friends reuniting after being separated by fate. Only, we weren't just good friends and what separated us wasn't fate. Or maybe it was; I'm still indecisive about this part. We keep the topic rolling around work, our new social circles, or sometimes updates about our mutual friends from university.

Even after almost a decade, Ethan is still the same guy I knew back then, except for the lighter skin that performs a line around his left ring finger.

"So, are you uh, married?"

Ethan glances at his own hand that has been resting on the table. "Yeah." He reflexively withdraws his hand as if he wants to hide it from my sight.

I never expected he would stay single after he left. But learning that he is now married while I'm still single, with no prospective boyfriend, gives me quite a punch in the face. I heard people tend to compete with their exes' life progress, and now I know that it's true.

"Oh, wow. Congratulations! I didn't know, I mean, you're not on Facebook or Instagram anymore, so, I didn't get the happy news at all."

"I know," Ethan mumbles and smiles. The smile that gave me strength every time I went through my rough patch. "I don't think those activities on social media benefit my future. Or maybe I just don't have time for that."

"I would imagine so." I take a sip of my tiramisu-flavored latte while my eyes still linger on his hand. "Where is your wedding band then?" I know I sound like a curious cat but I just can't help it.

"It's uh...I left it home," he answers with a dismissal tone, a sign that he doesn't want to talk about it.

I nod, deciding to drop it; it's not my business anyway. But I'm curious, capital C curious. Detaching my eyes from his finger, I stir my nearly-empty drink.

"What about you? Have you met someone special?"

I purse my lips. "A few yes, but none of them worked. You know how I am with relationships." I laugh, trying to break the small tension between us.

"Why don't I believe you?" He chuckles. "You were great, Char, and still are. And I don't think time will ever change that. I'm sure whoever the guy is, he needs to work so hard to deserve you."

Then why did you leave? Why didn't you want to be the guy who deserved me?

"Thanks," I mumble. "So, d'you have kids?"

Ethan shakes his head while tapping his fingers on his coffee cup. "Nope."

"Career first then family, huh? Still the ambitious Ethan I knew," I retort, earning a smile from him. Not a heartwarming smile, but it's more of a 'no comment' smile.

Ethan was always a private guy. It was one of the reasons why we often had arguments when we were still together; we had different ideas about how much we could share with others. It seems like he hasn't changed by keeping his life hidden. On the other hand, what happened eight years ago has gradually changed me and forced me to be more careful in sharing information with others. People say sometimes we just need a hard smack in the face to learn, and that's how I learn things in life. Well, I have to. For Chloe.

Right. Chloe. Ethan must have been under the impression I gave up my baby seven years ago. At least, that's what he learned before he disappeared from my life.

There is a brief silence between us before I drop the bomb.

"I kept the baby."

I have no idea why I told him that but it's too late to take it back. Ethan freezes. It takes him several seconds to finally move again.

"I thought you would give it up for adoption."

I shake my head. "I couldn't do it. I fell in love with my baby."

Ethan rubs his face before running his fingers through his hair. "I'm uh...you...damn, you have me speechless now, Char."

"I know. It doesn't sound like me, huh? I never wanted kids." A surge of warmth fills my heart when my mind jumps to Chloe. "Now, here I am. I can't imagine how my life would be without her."

Ethan's lips curl up into a smile. A genuine smile. "And a daughter! She must look a lot like you; mini Charlotte. How adorable."

Chloe's pellucid green eyes and her wavy chestnut hair flashes in my mind. "You would be surprised."

Chapter 9

This uncertainty wears me off more and more every day. By the time I leave work, I don't have enough energy to deal with my little chatterbox at home. I'm always late arriving at Sophie's house and my daughter's already eaten dinner with her aunt and cousin. Clearly, Chloe isn't happy with this situation.

"When can we eat together again?" asks my daughter when I pack up her lunch while she's finishing her cereal. "You're always late now."

"I know. Let's hope it will change soon."

"I don't like your new office. I like Dave's better."

I chuckle as I put her meal box, fruit, and drinking bottle into her lunch bag. "Of course you like my old company better. Dave always bribed you with a box of candy every time he needed me to work overtime."

Chloe grins, showing her bunny front teeth and a missing tooth next to them. "I have an idea. Why don't you call him to ask if you can work for him again?"

"Oh? Why?"

Chloe shrugs. "So that you can be home early, cook dinner, and eat with me."

My heart clenches as a guilty feeling creeps in. Making a mental note that I will talk about this to Mr. Knight, I turn around to face her. My hands clutch the edge of the granite countertop while I lean on it. "I'm sorry for not having time lately, sweetie. I promise I'll make it up when this is over."

"When will it be over?"

I bite the inner part of my cheek, not sure what to answer. Today, I will hear more about the result of yesterday's interview. With the last drop of faith I have for my CEO, I'm still hoping for a miracle, that a candidate has been selected. "It will be over as soon as they find someone who can do what I'm doing at work right now. Then I can go back to my normal job again. I'm not sure when, but I hope it will be next week."

Chloe knits her eyebrow. "Normal job?" Her eyes twinkle as her smile grows bigger. "Does it mean you're going to work for Dave again?"

"No." I shake my head, thinking about how to explain this work stuff for a seven-year-old to understand. "I can't go back to my old company, sweetheart. I have to stay in my current office. But at the moment, I need to do a different job for my big big boss," I emphasize the word big. "And when it's done, I will go back to the same job I did at Dave's company. Only, my new boss's name is going to be Max. And it means, I will have more time for us again."

"Okay." Chloe scrunches her face. "I don't like your big big boss."

"Oh? Why is that?"

"He sounds mean because he makes you go home late and tired every day." She drinks the rest of the milk directly from the bowl, before wiping her mouth with the back of her hand.

I feel a tug in my heart. If she only knew.

Lately, the idea of Chloe being my CEO's daughter is getting harder to ignore. I can't push the thought to the back of my mind anymore. Especially after I did my homework to check Ashton Knight's background. He was taking his doctoral program at the very university when the frat party took place. But still, there is no solid proof that the guy I slept with was really him. Did he even go to the party that night?

And even if he was the guy, what would I do exactly? Telling him about the daughter he never knew existed? Would the news surprise him or scare him shitless? Would he not want to have anything to do with Chloe once he found out? Or would he demand shared custody? Aarrgh. My head is spinning every time I think of all these scenarios.

For now, I will just look for some more evidence while focusing on my work transition.

"You know what? I have a terrific idea," I say as I wiggle my eyebrow. "Let's go to the movies tomorrow. After that, we can go to your favorite arcade. Then, we can drive to Sandy's house and eat pizza until we pass out. What do you say?"

Chloe's eyes instantly go wider in excitement. "Yes, please! And ice cream!"

I laugh and bob my head. "I'll call Sandy. She's been asking us to spend the weekend in her beach house."

Before Chloe can reply, the honk of her school bus blares from the street. Chloe jumps out of her seat and grabs her bags. After giving me a quick hug and kisses, she dashes to the door while squealing, "I can't wait for tomorrow!"

Leaning back against my seat headrest, I glance at the empty desk in front of Mr. Tan's room. Tanya left two hours ago because she has to work tomorrow. We have an important lunch meeting, and she will be the one who is in charge of the documentation. I'm glad they didn't assign me because of my status as a temporary secretary, otherwise, Chloe would raise hell.

Carefully massaging my shoulder, I close my eyes. A moan escapes my lips as the tension gradually leaves my muscle. Sitting behind the computer and straining my eyes for hours is definitely not the best idea to spend Friday afternoon. But I'm determined to get all these documents done before five and prepare for my exit on time. I need my weekend.

My mind jumps to the conversation I had with Chloe this morning and her bright eyes when she heard about our plan for tomorrow. The thing about being a mom is that when you see your child happy, it directly affects your own mood. I never knew how strong parents' feelings for their kids were until I had my own. That's how I actually started to accept my parents' flaws in raising me. They knew what they know, but it didn't mean they loved me any less.

"At least somebody is ready for the weekend." A deep voice pulls me back to the current moment. The scent that has become familiar invades my nostrils.

I open my eyes and a pair of green eyes are staring at me, prompting me to straighten my sitting position. "And who would that be, sir?"

"The very person who was just moaning and grinning in her seat," he replies before plopping down on my desk.

I unconsciously lean back again, creating as far as space between us. While doing my job in the past two weeks, having physical contact with him or staying in dangerous proximity was inevitable, but it was all under professional circumstances. And now, it doesn't feel like one. The smirk on the corners of his lips and the mischievous glaze in his eyes are evidence.

"I was just–"

"Thinking about the plan for the weekend. I know."

I open my mouth before closing it again. Then I shrug. "You're right. I did think about it just now."

"Of course I'm right. Let me guess. A candlelight dinner in a five-star restaurant with a potential suitor, who might propose during the dessert by hiding a huge diamond ring inside an overpriced chocolate mousse."

I chuckle. "Tempting. Girls would kill to have that kind of proposal. But alas, my weekend will be far from romantic, sir."

He raises his eyebrow slightly. "Too bad. Anyways, I have good news for you. I guarantee it's going to be better than a romantic proposal."

To be honest, I don't trust his judgment about the so-called good news. But I play along. "I'm intrigued."

"We have a new executive assistant."

"Oh, wow! What excellent news!"

"Yes, indeed. But," he pauses, causing me to hold my breath, "he needs two weeks to resign from his current work."

"Oh."

"Yep. Oh." He nods. "Thus, you'll be needed for another two weeks."

"Oh." I shudder.

"I thought you liked this role." He raises his eyebrows. "I still remember you said that it's such a valuable opportunity."

"I know. But..." I rake my brain to find a smart line to wriggle myself out of the coming trap. "It means I will be here for four weeks. What about my probation target? Six months is barely enough, and now I only have five months left."

"We're going to make a few adjustments to the contract."

Another two weeks of working in this hell hole makes me shiver. "Can I refuse this... generous offer?"

He purses his lips, a wicked glint flashing in his eyes. "You can." He then bites his lower lip, urging me to look away from the distracting view. "But I wouldn't do it if I were you."

I swallow. Is he doing what I think he is doing now? Is he finally playing the ghost chili card to prolong my torment? He'd better not.

"Is this a threat, sir?" My trembling voice betrays my attempt to stay brave.

"Why would I do such a thing, Ms. Garnett? What do I have against you?" he asks with a dangerously low tone. His green orbs are fixed on mine, piercing the last layer of courage I'm holding for dear life.

We lock our gaze for a while as the tension between us grows thicker.

"Ashton!" The staring contest between Mr. Knight and me is disrupted by the voice of our CFO's. We both turn our heads to look at Mr. Tan who is striding toward us with his phone in his hand. "We've got a little problem."

Mr. Knight props himself up from my desk. "What problem?"

"I just got a call. Tanya had an accident on her way home."

"What?" I shriek. "Is she alright?"

"Luckily, yes. Just a dislocated shoulder and some bruises. But she can't leave the hospital for twenty-four hours for observation."

"Thank god," I mumble.

Mr. Tan nods. "Yes, I'm also glad that it's nothing serious." He shifts his gaze to Mr. Knight. "But then we need someone to handle the meeting prep and to take minutes tomorrow."

Just like a helpless antelope in the Sahara, I whimper when the two lions slowly turn their gazes to me. I wish I could turn my desk into tall bushes where I can hide from their scrutinizing stares. I'm doomed.

"I-I can't. I have a plan for tomorrow. I promise my kid to bring her–"

"You have a kid?" Mr. Knight cuts me.

"Yes, I do."

"Can you ask her father to babysit her for an hour?" Mr. Tan asks.

"No, he's not...around."

"Can you ask someone else, your parents maybe? Or your friends? It's only a forty-five-minute meeting. We won't steal more than sixty minutes of your time tomorrow. Tanya has all the documents prepared and the lunch catering set."

I open and close my mouth like a clownfish gasping for water. I want to refuse but I feel somehow obligated to help. Have I started having an emotional bond with this job? No. Capital no.

"And we'll pay you extra for this. Doubled overtime rate," Mr. Tan goes on, earning a glare from Mr. Knight. "Plus lunch allowance, of course. And transport money."

My CEO scowls deeper, a faint grunt escaping his throat.

"I don't know. What time is the meeting?" I ask, beginning to consider it. Yeah, I'm cheap like that. Sue me.

"Twelve thirty."

I purse my lips. "I'll try to call around, to see if someone can babysit my girl."

"How old is she?" asks Mr. Tan.

"Seven."

"Ah, you can bring her along if you like. I'm sure Tanya ordered plenty for lunch. She can eat and wait in Ashton's room, watching cartoons or something."

"My room isn't a playground," Mr. Knight says, almost growling.

"Oh, it's clearly not. The girl won't like your dull room either. But at least you have a sofa for her to rest if she wants to nap."

My breath hitches in my throat when the thought of Chloe meeting Mr. Knight pops up in my head. It's not that I'm against it, but will I be ready to answer all questions when Chloe picks up the similarities between her and my CEO's physical appearance? Maybe I'm reading too much into this. Maybe no one will even notice.

"That can be arranged," I murmur.

Mr. Knight slips his hands into his pockets. The never-ending frown on his face is evidence that he doesn't like the idea at all, but he finally sighs in defeat. "Fine. But, no breaking stuff and no littering. Also, no leaking on the sofa or the carpet. Make sure her diaper isn't full."

"She's toilet trained, sir," I seethe, earning a laugh from Mr. Tan.

"Don't mind our CEO, Miss Garnett. He's clueless when it comes to children. He hates them."

"I don't hate children. I just don't like them because they tend to make a mess," Mr. Knight grumbles.

I smile sweetly. "Believe me, sir, if my girl wants to make a mess, it's not going to be your room."

Chapter 10

As the elevator bell dings and the doors slide open, I stride to the pantry while Chloe's little feet are hot on my heels. She needs to run a little to keep up with my speed. When I see John standing by the counter, busy arranging the food on the service trolley, I let out a relieved sigh.

"Oh, John! I thought no one was here when the caterer delivered the package. You really are our savior!" I beam as I walk to the trolley to check the meal for the lunch meeting. Two big platters full of sushi rolls and four different sauces are arranged in the middle of it, a platter of Japanese fried snacks, a gigantic bowl of mixed salad, and some beverages. My stomach rumbles as a result.

"Of course, miss–"

"I told you to call me Charlie."

"Charlie. Tanya texted me about the accident. Poor girl. She should take a taxi or get a driver for herself. I always wonder how she got her driver's license...Uh, hullo there, little one." John grins when his eyes spot Chloe who is hiding behind me and poking her head out, probably checking where all this delicious smell comes from.

"Hello."

"I'm John. What's your name?"

Chloe scoots to my side and shyly extends her hand. "Chloe. It's nice to meet you, sir John."

John laughs and takes her small hand. "Nice to meet you too, Madame Chloe."

I chuckle witnessing their encounter. I have no idea why Chloe always addresses men at my work as sir, except for Dave, of course. He and his wife are huge fans of my girl, and their boy happens to be Chloe's classmate.

"Alright. I'm going to get ready for the meeting," I say as I glance at the clock. "We still have twenty minutes until the meeting starts."

"I'll be at your service shortly, Madame," John bows at her before shifting his gaze to me. "Where do I deliver her lunch?"

"She will be in Mr. Knight's room," I reply, ignoring his exaggerated gasp. "Thank you for doing this, John."

With that, I grab my daughter's hand, ushering her to leave the pantry room. I can hear a reluctant groan escape Chloe's throat, but she needs to wait a bit for food. She has to be somewhere else right now and I've been anxious about this the whole morning.

Chloe is meeting her maybe daddy.

I keep convincing myself that there is nothing to worry about. No one knows what's going on inside my head. No one has learned my suspicion of who Chloe's father is. And it's all just speculation for now. Nothing has been proven yet.

Mr. Knight is sitting on his desk, eyes fixed on the phone in his hand, when I knock on his open door. "Good afternoon."

The man who is wearing a casual navy suit lifts his gaze from the cellular phone and his green irises lock with mine. He opens his mouth, about to say something, but immediately closes it again when his eyes catch a movement behind my hips. He knits his eyebrows as my daughter's face emerges. That's when the two pairs of emerald orbs meet, gawking at each other.

I hold my breath in anticipation. The situation reminds me of a scene in a Mexican telenovela my mom used to watch. When something big takes place, the camera switches from one face to another face, zooming in and out, suspenseful music blaring in the background. This is exactly that. Only, there is no camera and no suspenseful music since what we hear right now is the song Do You Want to Build a Snowman coming from the television screen.

I clear my throat. "This is Chloe, my daughter." I wrap my hands on Chloe's shoulders and give her a gentle push so that she takes a few steps forward. My eyes never leave my boss's which are now glued to my daughter's figure. "I'm going to get her settled first then I'm all set for the meeting."

Noticing that the pairs are still having a staring contest, I softly brush Chloe's chestnut bangs backward as I bend over to her ear. "What do you say when you meet a new person?"

As if being woken up from deep slumber, Chloe jerks her head and blinks. "Hello, sir. My name is Chloe. It's nice to meet you."

Mr. Knight props himself up from his desk and gives Chloe a tight smile. "Likewise. And I'm Ashton." He then walks to the sofa where I see children's books piling up on the coffee table, and a few puzzle boxes are arranged next to them. A jar of candies, which I swear wasn't there yesterday, sits in the middle of it. "Daniel brought these for your daughter. He said she can have them if she wants because his kids are now too big to keep this stuff."

"Oh, wow!" I gasp before nodding at Chloe who looks up at me, asking for permission. "Very generous of him. I need to thank Mr. Tan personally for this," I say while eyeing my eager daughter.

"Can she read?" Mr. Knight asks when he sees Chloe pick up a Cinderella book.

I shoot him an 'are you serious?' glare. First, diapers, now this. Was he born as a teenager?

He stares back at me and shrugs. "I don't have kids. And I don't study the phases of children's development."

"I can read books, but only the ones with lots of pictures," Chloe answers proudly before grinning like a mule eating briers. "Your eyes are also green, like mine! Or are they contact lenses? Mine are real though."

Mr. Knight frowns. "Why would I wear contact lenses?"

"To change your eye color?"

"But why?"

"To look cool. K-pop boys wear that. They also wear high heels like mama's she-letto!" Chloe's eyes widen in excitement. "Diana keeps a lot of pictures of them."

"Come again? Who is wearing your mom's high heels? Who's Diana?"

"Okay! Time for a meeting," I cut in. This conversation isn't going anywhere, and the meeting starts in less than fifteen minutes now. "Chloe, we will be just a few doors away. It's the last door down the hallway. If you need anything, go look for Sir John in the pantry–"

"Sir John?" Mr. Knight asks, but before I answer him, he seems to be able to connect the dots. "Oh!"

"If it's urgent, you can always come to me. Okay? Your lunch will be here soon." I glance at the jar of colorful sweets. "And no candy before lunch."

"Yeah, okay."

"We won't be long. I will be back before Elsa's movie is finished."

"Then we go to the arcade?"

"Yep."

"Okay. Have fun!" With that, she throws herself to the sofa and snuggles between the decorative pillows, hugging the book she picked to her chest.

What I love about how things work in this company is efficiency. They trim off the unnecessary social convo, which means it cuts down the chance to ass-lick. All issues are broken down into a clear concept map before they start listing the potential problem-solving. In the last ten minutes, they wrap it up by deciding which department is going to execute it. The only thing that slows down the meeting today is the food. But I don't mind, because I'm hungry as well, and the sushi roll is like a bomb on my tongue.

At twenty-past one, the meeting is over but people still linger. Seeing that I can't do my job when the room is still packed, I excuse myself to check on Chloe. To my surprise, the girl is now curling and purring on the yellow sofa, eyes closed while the movie is still playing. She rarely falls asleep in foreign places. Did John feed her a bit too much? Or was she tired out of boredom?

Tiptoeing, I take a blanket from the basket next to the sofa and spread it over my daughter carefully, not wanting to wake her up. I'm not sure how soon Mr. Knight needs to use his room again, but for now, I'll let her be. I can just carry her to the car once I'm done tidying up the meeting room.

When I'm back in the meeting room, there are only three people left. Max, Mr. Tan, and Mr. Knight are engrossed in a casual chat about their youth and reminiscing about the good old days. Well, it's about them being stupid, to be precise.

"How is your girl holding up? Did she manage to throw all our CEO's furniture out of the window?" Max asks when he sees me enter the room.

"Actually, she's asleep right now." I glance at Mr. Knight. "If you need to be in your room, I'll wake her up."

"No. Let the girl sleep a bit more," Mr. Tan replies on our CEO's behalf. "Ashton can use a little boy talk with us here. He needs to get his mind off work a bit."

Glancing at Mr. Knight who just shrugs at Mr. Tan's answer, I nod. "Ah okay. I'll get the rest of my job done then." With that, I go straight to inspect every table but my ears are at their maximum radar.

"Man, being a dad to a daughter is terrifying. I mean, we know how hormonal teenage boys are and the thing they do to get into girls' pants. We've been there!" Max whines. "I swear, if one of those kids dares to mess with my girl, he will be six feet under before his balls are fully grown."

Mr. Tan chuckles bitterly. "Max, prepare yourself for what is yet to come, boy. Very soon, you will be your daughter's unwanted fashion advisor." Mr. Tan piles up the papers in front of him while shaking his head. "Teenagers nowadays are showing too much skin. It's worrisome."

Max groans as he slumps back on his chair.

"One of the reasons I never want to have a kid," says Mr. Knight flatly. "I just don't wanna deal with all these teenage hormonal impulses and the bouncing rages. I'm not sure if I can deal with the mini-me, let alone having a daughter. I would probably tie her with a rope so that she's always in my sight."

I can't help scoffing, followed by a roar of laughter from Mr. Tan.

"And she will hate you for the rest of her life," the CFO retorts.

"Better than seeing her getting knocked up at a young age."

"That's what condoms are for."

"Don't trust it. It still can break."

"Speaking from experience, huh?" Mr. Tan laughs again. "Did she really never show up again?"

Mr. Knight chuckles before shaking his head. "Nope. Good thing. It means she didn't get pregnant."

"Wait, what? I don't get it," Max cuts in. "Did you say that you possibly impregnated a girl, and she let the chance to drag you into legal marriage slip off just like that?"

"It happened when I was still in university. She didn't know me."

"Ah, that makes sense!" Max clicks his tongue.

"Had a shitty day, hit a party, found a random pretty girl, and got laid. The next morning, I realized my condom broke, but she left already." Mr. Knight winces. "Man was it messy. I had to take a test to make sure I was clean and get mentally ready if she came back to me with a baby bump drama and stuff. The waiting was torture, but she never reappeared at any of those frat parties afterward. So, I assumed there was no baby after all."

"If your assumption was wrong, and she was actually pregnant, your child would be seven years old now, I think. Or maybe eight," Mr. Tan adds.

Mr. Knight purses his lips. "Yeah."

"Ah, the same age as Charlotte's girl!" Max exclaims.

It's when the documents in my hand slip off my grip and are instantly scattered all over my feet.

Chapter 11

It has been a week of torture. I don't know what to do with the newfound fact that Ashton Knight is actually the guy in that frat party. It's hard to think clearly since he has been hovering around my space lately, physically and mentally. And no, it's nothing romantic. This freaking temporary work is an absolute moron since it's more a job for two instead of one! That stingy asshole. I have to make sure Chloe doesn't inherit that trait.

"With all due respect, sir. How will I get all these reports, confirmation emails, and meeting preparation done in forty minutes?" I frown when my boss tells me about the internal meeting being moved to the morning slot. "The last time I checked, I still had two hands and ten fingers."

"By stop counting your body parts and do your job of course," Ashton Knight answers with his stoic face, eyes still on the paper in his hand.

I let out a deep breath, feeling defeated. With the pile of papers I need to shred by the end of the day, I trudge out of the room. Then his voice stops me.

"And Charlotte, can you stay back a bit this evening? The meeting with Mr. Remington starts a bit later today, and I'd like you to be around in case I need something.""

"I'm sorry but I can't today."

"Why not?"

"I promised Chloe I would be home on time tonight. For once."

Ashton raises his eyebrow. "Doesn't she have a nanny?"

I would snort if I didn't remember he was my boss. That kind of thing does not exist in my family. My mom will make sure Chloe is taken care of by a family member or a family friend she can trust while I'm away. She's always so nervous about how the world has become and how pedophiles are lurking around to target kids. Sophie and I even had to argue with Mom when we decided to send our kids to a public school.

"Unfortunately, no. Since I always got home late in the past few weeks, she had to stay with my sister until her bedtime. But today I need to pick her up on time." I hug the files against my chest while biting the inner part of my cheek. "I will make sure you will have all the files ready. The ones that you possibly need, too, to be on the safe side."

This is the first time I say no straight to his face. For a brief moment, I'm sure he's going to pull the ghost chili card again, but the man just stares at me for a few seconds, and then he nods. "Very well. That'll work."

Okay, I'm not expecting that. How does he give up that easily? Isn't he the infamous Knight who is good at pushing his staff members to the edge of their sanity? Or did he get up on the wrong side of the bed this morning?

Or maybe, just maybe, he is becoming soft because I've mentioned Chloe? Does Chloe have effects on him already? Does he even suspect anything? No, there is no way he knows that he has a daughter. I'm reading too much into this.

I know I need to tell him eventually. He has a right to know. Chloe has a right to know. But how do I approach this situation? How do I even begin? Maybe when I bring in his 10 A.M coffee next time, I can say, "Your coffee, sir. And oh, did you know that today's fun fact is about a broken condom?" Or maybe something like, "Your expresso, sir. I hope it's strong enough for you to carry on with the rest of your day after you hear this."

And what about Chloe? How will I bring the news that will change her life forever? She grew up believing that her father was my college sweetheart, Ethan Watkins. How does it change to Ashton Knight in one night? And now that her ghost father has come back from the dead, it might complicate things even more. Especially after I agreed to have another lunch with him, again.

Yes, I'm meeting Ethan today. And yes, I still remember that he's married. It's just a friendly lunch considering we're just two friends who share our past and try to reconnect —again, as friends, especially after the bitter state we had when we parted. Or maybe I just need closure even though I'm not sure if it's still relevant to our current situation. We both have moved on, right?

"Hey, Char, a little change for today's plan. Meet me at the Mexican restaurant instead of at the coffee shop. I have everything set up; the reservation is under my name. And, I will be tied up in a client meeting in the next few hours. I might not be able to answer a text or a phone call. See you there at lunch," Ethan's voice message plays on my phone, and I sigh. I know why he didn't tell me sooner about the change of venue; he wants to make sure I don't have room to wriggle myself out of the arrangement. Yep, definitely the same Ethan.

Once I'm done with my list-to-do before lunchtime, I grab my bag and head to that old stucco building at the corner end of this business district. It stands out against those tall buildings yet the city decided to keep it for some reason. I've been told that the restaurant has been there even before this area was turned into a business center, way before I was born into this world.

Ethan hugs me and gives me a peck once I arrive. It was innocent, but his scent throws me back to the old days when he was still the center of my universe. It feels so foreign now, yet it awakens something in me that has been buried for so long. The familiarity. The nostalgia.

After we order our meals, we start with a light convo about our weeks. Talking to him is always easy, something I missed the most from us. We jump from one topic to another effort-lessly, and once he starts asking about my daughter, the devil is out of its lease. I will never get enough of telling people about my girl. What can I say? I'm a proud mother.

"I'd love to meet Chloe someday," Ethan says, his eyes twinkling as the words escape his lips.

"You would?" I ask, a bit taken by surprise. I mean, he's married and we used to be lovers. Meeting his ex's daughter will be a little bit scandalous, won't it? Because it means we need to make another appointment to meet up. What will his wife think about this? Or will he bring her along? Ugh, I don't even want to think about how awkward it will be.

"Of course. She's your daughter; she's important to you."

"Okay," I reply, trying hard not to read too much into his answer. He's just being nice, right?

Ethan is still not wearing the ring, and my curiosity is through the roof right now, but asking him again isn't an option. The last time we met, he sent the message loud and clear that he didn't want to talk about it. And since he's been avoiding the very topic today, I know enough to shut up and swallow the lump of curiosity that is stuck in my throat.

Our next topic revolves around how he started his career after graduation. His mother, sadly, passed away in the same year of his graduation and it was when he started his new life in this city, met his wife, and got married. But the way he keeps dodging my questions about his wife is killing me. It urges me to keep glancing at his left ring finger now and then. I swear I don't do it deliberately because I don't want to make things weird, but I just can't help myself.

And of course, Ethan notices that. He rubs his ring finger with his thumb as he purses his lips. "We're going through a divorce right now."

The fork slips off my fingers, creating a sharp clinking sound when it hits the plate. "Sorry. What did you say?"

Ethan sighs, the hurt now visible in his eyes. "Our marriage has been rough since we lost our son a few years ago. We agreed that it's time to call it a day."

"Oh, Ethan..."

"The death of our child drifted us apart. After a series of marriage counseling, we just can't go back to where we started it. Maybe we both just can't get past the mourning state." His jaws clench as he explains further, and I know it's uncomfortable for him to share this.

My mouth opens and closes a few times but I can't muster any words. If anything, Ethan deserves to be happy after what life has thrown at him in the last several years. My heart aches for him, feeling his pain. No parents should see their children die. In silence, I extend my hand and wrap my fingers around his, answered by him squeezing them back.

"Thanks, Char. We did try. Very hard. But it's just... not there anymore," he mumbles. "And it's a good thing that we bumped into each other again. It's something they call divine intervention, maybe?"

I smile at him as an answer.

Chapter 12

Days go by and I'm still clueless about what to do with Chloe and her undisclosed father. I told Sandy about my discovery during our visit to her beach house two weekends ago. She was as dumbfounded as I was, but Sandy was Sandy. She quickly got back to her rational mind.

"Talk to him, tell him whatever it is. It's nothing like eight years ago when you were a scared kitten, looking for support from someone who knocked you up," she said. "You will just offer him the fact that Chloe is his child. He doesn't have to be involved with his daughter's life. He doesn't even have to worry about child support because look at you, you're doing just fine raising her alone. The bottom line is, you don't keep this important fact from him."

We had moved Chloe to the guest room so that Sandy and I could catch up in the living room without having to whisper all the time. "But he's my big big boss. Don't you think it will be super awkward?"

"I bet."

"Maybe I should search for another job before dropping the bomb. Because if things get weird, or even worse, he denies Chloe and creates a drama out of it, my career is on the line."

"Do you think he will deny Chloe?"

"I don't know, Sand." I sighed. "He doesn't want kids, let alone a daughter. He might not take this news well, or get panicked, or whatever. I really don't know how he will react to this. So, having another job for a backup if things get ugly sounds reasonable at the moment."

Sandy never said she agreed or disagreed with my idea, but knowing me, she understood why I wanted to deal with this at my own pace. I know I've improved a lot in these past years, but I'm still that girl who jumps from one impulsive decision to another impulsive one. Thus, I've decided to wait until I'm done with the temporary position. Not seeing him on a daily basis will probably help me think more clearly.

And the big day has arrived; today is my last day working on the executive floor.

The new guy, Andy, has finished his speedy employment training and starts his journey as Ashton Knight's assistant. Andy is around my age and looks enthusiastic about his new job, and I will not, at any cost, crush his spirit on his first day.

"Glad you made it to this floor today," greets Mr. Knight when he's back from a business event. "I'm sure Ms. Garnett has explained how things work in general. Feel free to ask me if you have further questions. And" —he shifts his gaze to me— "I've got something for you."

I raise my eyebrows, intrigued by his sudden friendliness. Something doesn't feel right. "Oh?"

After rummaging through the business event bag he's been carrying, he takes a galileo doll out and puts it on the assistant desk, next to the computer. "Well, it's more for Chloe. I heard she's into the solar system. The event was all about it and I thought she would love to have one." Seeing me speechless and gaping at him, he continues, "And it's also a part of my apology for making her mom stay later at work in these past few weeks."

"Oh, wow," I gasp when I can find my voice again. "She will definitely love this. She adores him. Thank you so much, sir." I beam at him. I have no idea he paid attention to my random chatter about Chloe lately, and the fact that he did makes me feel somehow happy.

He nods and looks back at Andy. "I will be in my room for the rest of the day. I believe it's going to be an easy day for all of us. While Ms. Garnett begins packing up, you can start digging into your work." With that, he strides away and disappears behind his door.

"Wow!" Andy blinks as he brushes back his jet-black hair, his dark eyes shining in amazement. "We're so lucky to have a charismatic, generous, and thoughtful boss!"

I almost choke but I muffle it with a fake cough. "Yeah. You're so blessed to get this job, you know. He's definitely one of a kind."

I grin from ear to ear on my way home knowing I don't have to go back to the thirteenth floor on Monday. Andy might hate me one day when he learns about Ashton Knight's true character, but I will worry about it another time. For now, I will just enjoy being lazy with Chloe in our matched pajamas for the whole weekend, except for a couple of hours when I'm meeting Ethan for lunch.

I know I wasn't in the right mind when I agreed to this. When he asked to meet me for dinner, I said no, but I couldn't turn him down completely. Then we settled on having lunch. At least, it feels less intimate. Ethan lives alone and when he's not working, he'd rather go outside to meet friends, or just drive somewhere, anywhere but home. It's sad to see him like this and it feels like I should be there for him in his time of need. I guess I still care for him.

We meet up on Saturday afternoon at the busiest cafe in my town square since Ethan doesn't want me to drive all the way to the city. Just like at our other lunch meet-up, we keep everything light and easy, staying away from depressing topics while enjoying our coffee and pastries.

When our plates and cups are almost empty, my phone rings. I hold my breath when I see the name flashing on my phone screen.

"Soph, is everything okay?" I ask once I pick up the phone.

"We're here!" Sophie squeaks loudly, matching the blaring music in the background, making me wince and slightly distance the phone from my ear. "I gave up. Diana wouldn't stop nagging me until I brought her to the bookstore. Chloe didn't want to stay in, too. So, here we are." She chuckles, sounding a bit too giggly.

"Gosh, Soph, for a second I thought there was something wrong with Chloe." I let out a sigh of relief.

"Oh, no. Chloe is absolutely fine. Are you still at Maura's Cafe? Listen, we're going to pop up there. The girls want to grab some bubble tea and then we're out of your hair."

"Yeah, I'm still here," I reply, glancing at Ethan who is frowning at his phone screen. A realization dawns on me like a brick hitting my skull. "What? You guys are coming? No–"

"Why not?"

Seeing Ethan's head snap and his eyes now on me with curiosity, I gulp. "It's..." Shit. Ethan can't hear me saying that Chloe shouldn't be here, meeting his ghost daddy. "It's busy here. Very busy. I think you guys better grab the tea some- where else."

Granted, my answer prompts Ethan to look at our sur- roundings. He frowns as he sees the cafe is half empty since lunchtime is over.

"Umm, Char. We are here," Sophie replies.

"What? Oh–" I stop abruptly before turning around in hor- ror just to find the trio entering the cafe, a paper bag hanging on each hand as they grin widely at me.

"Mama!" Chloe squeals and throws herself at me.

Once her warm body snuggles in my arms, her scent soothes me, but not enough to calm my nerves at this very moment. It's when a paper bag hits my calf. I glance down and frown. "Now, what did Aunt Sophie get you?" I ask.

Chloe and I go to the bookstore once a month so that she can pick what she likes. And the last one was just a week ago.

Sophie waves her hand in a dismissive gesture, probably feeling guilty for breaking our deal to not over-pamper our kids. "Just a Disney magazine and some do-books. No biggie."

"Soph–"

"Oh, gosh. Ethan?" Sophie gasps, glancing at me in surprise. "I didn't know Char was meeting you for lunch."

"Sophie." Ethan stands up. Instead of shaking my sister's hand, he hugs her and gives her friendly pecks on the cheeks. "Long time no see."

"Damn right! It's been seven years...no, eight years!" Sophie replies, unaware of my eyes boring into her head. Doesn't she realize what is going on right now? I'm so close to spilling my drink onto her dress when she goes on, "How are you?"

"I'm fine, thank you. What about you?"

"Can't complain. Well, my husband is still working offshore, so it's just me with the girls for now. This is" —Sophie pulls Diana to her side— "my daughter, Diana. She was still a toddler the last time you saw her. And this is" —Sophie's other hand holds Chloe by the shoulders— "Chloe–" Sophie stops abruptly. Her eyes widen as a strangled noise escapes her throat.

"My daughter," I finish Sophie's line. "Girls, what do you do when you meet new people?"

Diana and Chloe take turns to come forward and shake Ethan's hand while murmuring, "Nice to meet you."

"I...uh...we're not staying. We're just going to grab our drinks and go," Sophie says with an overly wide smile plastered on her face. "Let's go, girls. Bubble tea time!" With that, Sophie walks to the counter with Diana hot on her heels, but Chloe doesn't budge from her spot.

When I turn my eyes to her, my daughter is taking the seat next to me, eyes fixed on the man in front of her. Something she always does to my potential date or boyfriend. If Ethan feels uncomfortable with her scrutinizing glare, he doesn't show it. Mimicking Chloe's gesture, he folds his arms and rests them on the table while staring back at her, smiling.

"You have beautiful eyes, Chloe," Ethan starts.

"Thank you. Mama said I have them from my dad."

"I see." Ethan nods, still smiling but it doesn't reach his eyes.

"So, Ethan, how did you meet my mama?"

Ethan raises his eyebrows in amusement. "We were friends back in university."

"Were you her college sweetheart?"

My breath hitches in my throat. Oh, shit!

Ethan chuckles before answering. "Yes, you can say that."

Shit, shit, shit! I haven't warned Ethan about this. "Chl–"

"So, you're Ethan Watkins. You're my dad."

"What?"

Ethan's eyes widen, caught by surprise as I bury my face in my hands, hoping the ground to open up and swallow me whole right now.

"Mama said my father is Ethan Watkins, her college sweetheart, who left her heartbroken and pregnant."

The only time I saw Ethan speechless was when I told him I was carrying a random guy's child in my belly. And right now, I'm witnessing it once again. His mouth hangs open and his eyebrows are knitted together as if he is trying to make sense of what Chloe just told him, scratch that, what the girl just accused him of.

"Chloe, you're barking at the wrong tree, sweetheart," I say, my voice squeaking like a mama duck. "This isn't Ethan Watkins, my ex-boyfriend."

The pair shift their gaze to me. Ethan raises his eyebrow, looking intrigued, while Chloe frowns in confusion.

"He is Ethanol...lan. Yes! Ethan Nolan." I shoot a glare at Ethan who almost snorts from laughing before shifting my eyes back to Chloe. "So, I dated two Ethans, Ethan Watkins and Ethan Nolan. And this Ethan is not your father."

"Ow." Chloe bites her lower lip, sheepishly turning her head back to Ethan. "I'm sorry. I'm mistake for someone else."

I would correct her grammar if we weren't in this awkward situation. So, I bite my inner cheek and let the conversation roll.

"No problem. That happens," Ethan replies.

Chloe doesn't take her eyes off him. "Now I understand why your eyes aren't green."

"Yeah, I wish I had them."

Chapter 13

After over a month, it was the first time I woke up and smiled brightly on Monday morning. Yes, I work on the fourth floor again today, where I belong. But that also means I need to decide soon how to break the news to Ashton Knight about the daughter he doesn't know exists. Especially after things got a bit messy last weekend with Chloe and Ethan.

Once the trio left the cafe, Ethan gave me a flat expression, a sign that he demanded an explanation. "I always refrained from asking you about the guy, Chloe's father, but since my name is somehow mentioned in the storyline, I would like to know what happened."

And I told him everything. Everything as in I couldn't bring myself to tell her that she wasn't made out of love, that I even thought of getting rid of her, and that telling lies was the easiest way out. The thing that didn't pop up in my head is every lie we tell incurs a debt to the truth. Sooner or later the debt needs to be paid.

Soon, Chloe and I need to sit down and have a very long talk about her true father's identity. It's time to tell her what really happened back then, as long as her seven-year-old brain can handle it. No more false stories; no more deception. But first, I need to know how her father reacts to the news because his reaction plays a big part in his disclosure to Chloe.

"Charlotte!" Shanti's high-pitched voice pulls me back to the current moment. Sebastian and the girls behind her grin widely as they find me in my cubicle. They must have just finished having their breaky in the pantry.

"Hi, guys! I'm back. Yay!"

Weirdly enough, as much as I wanted to be back here, I didn't feel that ecstatic when I saw my office space again, and it still feels strange sitting here in my cubicle now. The executive assistant desk has been my home in the past month, and despite the workload, I've grown some kind of emotional attachment to that spot. Maybe I just need time to get used to this floor.

"So, you survived the deadly voyage and now are back in one piece!" Gina says.

"Seems like it." I laugh as I lean back against my chair's headrest. "So, what's up? What have I missed?"

Gina shrugs. "Not much. Just the same shit different day. Well, lucky we have Shanti, our office gossip supplier. She makes our life a bit more colorful every day."

I chuckle as I bend over to turn on my PC. "So, what is the hottest and the newest gossip?"

Gina plops down on my empty desk. "You have probably heard it or seen it yourself. You've been on the thirteenth floor for a while."

I raise my eyebrows, my curiosity piqued. "Okay? I'm not sure if I'm following, though."

"It's about our big daddy," Shanti replies, wiggling her eyebrows. "Didn't you hear the gossip about him going around lately?"

"Well," I mumble as I wrinkle my nose. "I'm sure there are lots of things about him to gossip about. Which one are we talking about?"

"The juiciest one, of course, titled Mr. Knight's long-lost love is back."

"Huh?" A long lost what?

"His ex, the one he was dating for some time, is back in the picture. The girl from the payroll swore she saw him and his ex having a candlelight dinner last week. They looked so much in love, she said. But, oh well, I never liked that chick. I don't know if I'm going to ship them."

For some reason, I feel my stomach churn, but I try to ignore it. This news has nothing to do with me. Right? "Oh, is this the ex that was once an assistant executive in this company?"

Shanti's eyes widen in excitement. "Ah, you've learned about the real company history, I see. I know you're smarter than you let on."

Sebastian breaks into laughter before shaking his head in amusement. "I didn't know that keeping up with office gossip requires a brain cell."

"What are you talking about?" Shanti smacks him on the shoulder. "Of course it needs one. Just like when we go to war, we have to learn about the battlefield. Who is who, what is what, and where is where. And this office, my dear, is a battlefield for all of us. Remember, ignorance is bliss but knowledge is power, and it's true."

Sebastian throws both his hands up in the air, a sign of defeat, yet he's still chuckling. "Okay, okay! You girls win. I'm out of here. Going to talk to Max. And Char, you're coming with me to a client meeting today, right?"

It takes a few seconds for my brain to register his question. "Oh, yeah, I am. Let me uh, quickly learn about the client's company profile."

And nothing I read on my computer screen goes to my head. All I can see is Ashton Knight having a romantic dinner with a faceless woman, holding her hand and talking about their future. Another jab hits my gut. Why does this even bother me?

Is it because his rekindled relationship will affect Chloe's arrival into his life? No, of course not. If anything, his daughter's disclosure may affect his relationship because it's going to change his whole game as a human and a social being. But why do I feel this tightness in my chest?

"Fuck me," I mutter under my breath when I realize what's happening.

The reason I'm not that ecstatic about being back on the fourth floor is him. I can't see him that often anymore. I can't poke his nerves or have a stupid banter with him when I feel like it. I can't gawk at him while pretending to listen to his instructions.

I'm attracted to Asston freaking Knight.

I've been thinking about this and have decided that it needs to wait a little bit. Instead of searching for a backup job, I chose to stay here, at Knight & Co., to prove to them that I meet the standards they set for their employees. Heck, I'm not only aiming for the standards, I'm striving for a new record. Then I can use it as my bargaining point when I send my CEO a friendly email titled "Exceptionally Important".

The thing is, thinking about Ashton Knight makes me nervous. Having a thing for him is just the ultimate recipe to create a double drama, and I don't want that. Plus, he is seeing someone now. This is the very reason I've been pushing the thought of him to the back of my mind and focusing on my job, hoping that the feeling will disappear by itself.

I believe it's just an impact of being held captive for weeks with no office social life. The living creature I interacted with most of the time was him even though I felt constantly intimidated by him. Maybe, this is what they call Stockholm syndrome, which is good that I haven't bumped into him since I left the executive floor. The time will shake away his effects on me.

The first-Monday-of-the-month meeting starts in five minutes. Knowing that I will see my former direct boss again gives me conflicted feelings. Admittedly, I'd love to see his handsome face again. But will that do any good for my sanity? Highly unlikely.

"Are you coming?" Sebastian gets up before snatching the blue suit that is hung over his chair's headrest.

"Yeah." Turning off my computer screen, I grab my phone and nervously catch up with him. "Did you know that Mr. Hanz tried to move the meeting schedule to Friday evening at a fancy restaurant this week?"

Sebastian snorts and shakes his head. "Of course he did. That womanizer bastard. What did you say?"

"I didn't directly say no, just nicely suggested we better keep it in a place where we can use a laptop, a flat white wall, and a laser pointer."

He cackles. "Good one!"

"Anyways–" A ringing tone from my phone stops my line. When I see Chloe's school number on my screen, I frown. "I need to take this. I'll be right behind you."

"Okay." With that, he strides ahead to the meeting room.

Feeling my heart drumming against my chest, I press the green button. "Good morning, Charlotte speaking," I greet as I lean back to the glass wall behind me, my hand clutching my phone a little bit too hard.

"Good morning, am I speaking to Chloe Ann Garnett's mother?" says a male voice from the other side of the line.

"Yes, it's her. May I know what this is about? Is Chloe alright?"

"Unfortunately, no. There was an accident in the street near the school involving a drunk driver and a school bus... and Chloe was in it–"

"No!"

"–she's now on her way to Grace hospital for an emergency–"

"I'm on my way!"

"Ms. Garnett, if you drive, please–"

I don't bother to listen to what he says next.

Chapter 14

The next scene is a blur. My surroundings freeze as I dash to grab my bag from my cubicle, sprint to exit the building, and run to the bus stop. With shaking hands, I scroll down my phone screen to find a taxi number while reading the bus timetable at the same time, thinking about which one will bring me faster to the hospital. In the next five minutes, I'm sitting in the backseat of a cab that miraculously showed up when I was still deciding. I can't take a train home anyway. Even though it will bring me faster to my town around this peak hour, my legs and brain would just refuse to function.

After I manage to call Sophie and leave a message for my boss, Max, I begin to usher the driver to go faster and faster. I groan when we have to slow down or stop at the traffic light and cuss every time we bump into another stupid driver.

"I understand that this is an emergency, Ma'am, but please, take a deep breath and calm down. I will take you there as fast as I can without causing another accident," says the driver in front of me, his dark irises eyeing me from the rearview mirror. Irritation and compassion coat his gaze.

The driver's line is like a slap in the face. He's right. I need to control my impulse that has gone through the roof now. I take a deep breath and close my eyes, but all I can see is Chloe's face and I whimper again. Leaning back against the headrest, my eyes are staring blankly at the car ceiling. And for the first time in my life, I say my prayer to all gods that might hear my desperation.

I jump when my phone rings, flashing Sophie's name on its screen.

"I'm in the hospital now. Chloe and all the kids are still inside, getting the emergency treatment, and we're not allowed to come in." Sophie is trying to talk in a calm manner but I know better that she is also shaken.

"Have you seen her? Is she alright? Is she awake?"

"No, I haven't seen her, Char. I'm not allowed to go inside, remember? I'm in the emergency waiting room now, sitting with other moms. I will update you as soon as I hear something. How far are you?"

"Not that far. I will be there in five or ten minutes tops."

"Okay. I will call Mom and Dad now." With that, Sophie hangs up, taking my last restraint from falling apart.

I break down and cry.

I whine to lessen the throbbing tightness in my chest. I just want to be with my baby now, holding her hand while she has to go through this painful process. Is she in pain now? Is she scared? Does she need her mama like every other night when she had a nightmare about zombies lurking around inside her wardrobe?

This is the point where I will do anything to make sure she's alright. This is the point where a mother is willing to give her life for her child.

"We're here, Ma'am." The driver's voice pulls me from my jumbled mind.

After I pay the taxi bill, without bothering to get my change, I sprint to the emergency room. Sophie welcomes me with a tight embrace and we cry together in each other's arms. We don't say a word because we know that all kinds of reassurance lines sound like bullshit right now. Chloe is like a daughter to her and she's as terrified as I am. What we can do is wait in silence, facing our fear together.

Other parents, whose kids were also on the same school bus, don't look anything better than we are. They sit on their chairs, fidgeting, faces as white as sheets, looking defeated. A few even sit alone and sob silently. I know it's not the right time to say it, but I'm so blessed to have a supportive sister who always shows compathy through my hard times.

After fifteen minutes which feels like forever, the emergency door swings open. A nurse, whose clothes have some bloodstains on, mentions a name, followed by a couple getting up and striding inside. The next thing I hear is an agonizing howl from the woman and we all know what that means.

A shiver runs down my spine. I have never been this scared in my life.

Minutes go by and it's excruciatingly slow. A few more names are mentioned, but none of them is my daughter's name. We wait and wait with the rest of the faith we have.

"Is the family of Chloe Garnett here?" asks the nurse who is standing at the end of the emergency hall.

"Yes!" Sophie replies as she pulls me up and herds me to the medical personnel who is now looking at us with an expression I can't decipher.

"How's she?" I ask but my voice comes out as a whisper.

"Let's talk about this inside. The doctor is waiting," the nurse answers before holding the door open for us.

The emergency room is in chaos. A strong smell of blood and the saturation of alcohol hits my nostrils. Through the gap between the white curtains, I see beds lining up and occupied by a few kids who are lying unconscious and hooked up to different kinds of wires. The health workers are moving back and forth, blocking my sight.

The nurse directs us to a small room covered only by a curtain where a middle-aged man in a white robe is waiting for us.

"Hello, I'm doctor Wayne, who handled your daughter." He shakes our hands. "First of all, I'm sorry for what happened to your little girl. This is a tragedy that costs us lots of pain, even lives." The doctor sighs. "Chloe is still unconscious, but from the test we've run, there are no signs of internal bleeding. Only, her shoulder joint is dislocated, and we are currently waiting for the x-ray result to see if there are any other conditions that we need to know before we proceed with further measures."

Hearing that Chloe survives brings back my ability to speak again. "Will she be alright, Doc?"

"That's what we hope. The thing is... she has a serious cut near her hip, causing her to lose a lot of blood and it's rather alarming. Unfortunately, we don't have enough supplies to give her a transfusion right now. We are calling around for help to see if other hospitals have the supply, but it might take hours, maybe days. However, if her biological parents are here, and are fit to be the donor, it will be so much faster for her to get the supply she needs, which means less risk of suffering from an organ or brain defect."

I take a sharp breath. "I don't have the same blood type as hers, but I sure can get a hold of her biological father."

"That would be great," Doctor Wayne replies. "How long do you think you can get him here?"

"Give me a few hours. But please, before I go, can I see my baby just for a second?" I beg.

"Of course. She is still in the observation room, you can see her from the outside. Tina will show you the way," the doctor replies, pointing at the nurse who let us in earlier.

I break into tears again when I see my daughter lying motionless on the hospital cot. Her tiny face is covered by a breathing tube while the IV fluid hangs on the pole next to her bed. The EKG machine is beeping next to her, showing green and red lines against its black screen. I want to see more than I can see now. How bad is her wound? Is she cold there? Is the hospital blanket warm enough?

"Char," Sophie mumbles as she nudges my shoulder. "About Chloe's biological father, did you mean it?"

I haven't told Sophie about Ashton Knight because I wanted to have my space to process all of this. Sophie is nothing like Sandy; her big sis complex would get the best of her and surely, it would drive me up the wall.

I nod weakly at her question. "Yes. I found him. I'm sorry I didn't tell you sooner, Soph. It's just..."

"No, don't worry about it. Go get him now. The sooner it is, the better it is for Chloe. I'll stay here to make sure she gets what she needs."

"Are you sure? What about Diana? Who's going to grab her from school?"

"Mom and Dad should be here soon. I can ask Dad to pick her up later. Just go, Char. Chloe needs the blood supply," Sophie urges.

I nod again. After glancing at my girl for one more time, I turn on my heels and leave the room. Hang in there, sweetheart. Mama will be back with the help you need.

Chapter 15

I 've been trying to call Ashton Knight's personal number, leave him a voice message, and even text him, but I haven't gotten a single response from him. Once I can get a hold of Andy, he says that his boss has been tied up in the meeting with Mr. Remington and the team. For dramatic effect, he whispers ominously on the phone, "If you still want to have your soul intact, you'd better not bother him now."

Honestly, I don't care. He can bite me all he wants later, but first, I want his blood.

It's already lunch break when I reach the thirteenth floor. Once the elevator doors slide open, the delicious aroma coming from the pantry invades my nostrils, making my stomach growl like a mad dog. But food can wait because my daughter's life is on the line. Noticing that the executive assistant's desk is empty, I march directly to Mr. Knight's door. Andy told me that our CEO didn't have any lunch appointments, which means he's probably having his lunch inside his room right now.

Once standing in front of his door, I take a deep breath while gathering my courage to announce my arrival. It's when I hear a male voice murmur and a female giggle behind the door. He's having company, and whatever they're doing at this very moment, it doesn't sound like a work-related visit. Is he doing funny business in his office room right now? During lunchtime?

The latest gossip about him getting back together with his ex pops up in my mind. It must be her then; it must be the faceless woman. If it wasn't for Chloe, I would just turn around and leave, but what needs to be done needs to be done.

The laughter stops once I knock, followed by a brief silence before his familiar voice echoes across the room. "Yes?" He must think I'm Andy.

Feeling unsure about how he will react to my unexpected appearance, I clear my throat and reply, "Mr. Knight?"

I hear footsteps approach the door and before I can respond, the door is swung open, revealing the face that has been giving me conflicted feelings in the past month. "Charlotte?"

"Sir," I greet, forcing myself to smile.

His eyes graze down observing my appearance which I'm sure looks like total shit right now. "What's wrong?"

"Can I have a word with you, sir?" I ask, glancing at the office room behind him but the door is blocking my sight.

"Can't it wait until the lunch break is over? I'm busy right now."

I shake my head while fiddling with the phone in my hand. "I'm afraid not, sir. It's urgent."

"Who is it, Ash?" asks the female voice before a red-haired woman emerges from behind him. Then our eyes meet.

She's pretty. No, she is stunning. Her ivory skin glows against her auburn hair, bringing out her breathtaking grayish-green eyes. Faint freckles adorn her high cheekbones, sprinkling over her pointed nose. She's not as tall as I am, but the way she carries herself reminds me of a catwalk model.

Mr. Knight turns his head to her and smiles, making me realize that he never actually smiled during the time I was working for him. Nothing like this. "It's my new account executive, Charlotte. She said she needed to talk."

The now not-faceless woman breaks our staring contest and looks up at her boyfriend, slightly frowning. "Does it have to be now?"

"Yes, actually. It has to be now," I interject.

Mr. Knight furrows his eyebrow as he tilts his head to me, showing a mix of surprise and annoyance; the expression he gives when someone answers for him. His lips twitch and the glint in his eyes throws me back to the first days I worked for him. The challenge glare. "Okay. You have sixty seconds to talk."

I stand still, gaping at him and then at his girlfriend, not sure how to deal with this situation. "I...need to talk in private."

"Now you have me curious. What kind of private thing that can not be spoken in front of me?" asks the woman, looking amused, contrasting the frown on Mr. Knight's face.

Feeling my agitation grow every second, I refrain from taking the bait. "Please, sir. This is very important."

Mr. Knight sighs. "Ms. Garnett, I gave you a chance to talk but you didn't take it. And this isn't a good time. Please come back after the lunch break." With that, he pushes the door closed, swallowing the sight of his girlfriend's curious face.

I see red. His wooden door has now turned crimson in my eyes as fire ignites in me. Before I can think of any consequences I will face later, I shout at him. "I swear if you don't hear me out, I'm not gonna forgive you. Ever!"

The next few seconds are thick with silence. All I can hear is my raging breathing and my heart thumping hard against my chest. Then the door in front of me is pulled open again.

"I beg your pardon?" he asks, his eyes as sharp as a knife, ready to chop me into pieces.

"For the whole month, sir, I worked for you against my will, abandoning my kid, and sacrificing my free time. Never ever did I complain or humiliate you for mistreating your staff. And when I really, really need you for once, you don't give me this," I growl, my hand clutching my phone furiously, holding the urge to bash someone's face, preferably the face that is gawking at me right now.

Ashton Knight looks taken aback by my outburst. "What are you talking about?"

I close my eyes and take a deep breath, refraining from screaming at his face. "I've been asking you to talk in private and please, just trust me, you don't want this to be heard by anyone else."

"Wait!" This back-and-forth starts to get on his girlfriend's nerves. "In case you don't know, Ashton and I are very very close. I don't think you two need to find somewhere private to talk. You can start talking now or come back later. We're wasting too much time on you alrea--"

"Dee," Mr. Knight cuts her, his eyes never leaving my face. "You have five minutes. If this is all just some kind of bullshit, you will regret pulling off this stunt. To the main meeting room. Now."

"Are you kidding me?" the girlfriend asks in a high-pitched tone, glaring at Mr. Knight.

"She worked for me for a month. When she says this is important, then this is important. I'll be back in five," he says before striding next to me and heading to the room at the end of the hallway. Once inside, he closes the door behind him while eyeing me pacing back and forth across the room. "Your five minutes start now."

I press my palms against both sides of my skirt, rubbing them up and down. "I need your blood."

There is a few seconds delay before he responds. "What?"

"Okay, I'll rephrase. Chloe had an accident this morning. She lost too much blood and she needs to have a blood transfusion as soon as possible. My blood type doesn't match hers. Therefore, I need you to donate your blood for her."

Ashton Knight stares at me in bewilderment as if he has to solve the most difficult algebra case in the world. "I'm so sorry to hear about your little girl. I do hope she's alright, but

I'm afraid I'm not following you. You need me to donate my blood for her? But, why? Don't they have supplies for that?"

"Unfortunately, no. Not for the time being. They're calling around now, but I need to be faster for this."

"But why does it have to be me?"

"Because you have the same blood type as Chloe's." A small voice in my head begins to spit out some doubts. What if it's not the case? What if he isn't the father despite all of the evidence?

"You don't even know my blood type."

"Yours is A negative, as well as Chloe's."

Ashton Knight drops his jaws. "How... what... how did you know?"

The moment of truth has arrived. "Because Chloe is your daughter," I answer as I close my eyes, feeling relieved, yet not daring to see his reaction.

One second, two seconds, three seconds, and I still haven't heard his response. I stop counting and decide to give him time to process.

"This...is a prank, isn't it? You know I won't appreciate any kind of bullshit, don't you?" he asks, prompting me to open my eyes, look him in the eye, and shake my head.

"No, sir, this isn't a prank. Why would I joke about something this serious?" I reply. "Chloe was conceived over eight years ago in a frat party before the Christmas break. I was drunk and not in the right mind when I crashed into the party. Then I bumped into a guy on the dance floor. He has a pair of beautiful emerald green eyes, and they drew me in. We then went up to one of the empty rooms and had sex. The next morning, when I realized what happened, I panicked and ran home. I believe I left my black scarf behind; the one that must have been used to tie me up. Well, I can't remember the details but I woke up with my scarf wrapping around my wrist."

The more I talk, the paler his face goes. He trudges back until he hits the door behind him. If I can make a movie out of what's going on inside his head right now, it will be like a fast backward scene until it stops on the night we met. The movie is now playing again, showing scene after scene in chronological order, exactly how I told him a few minutes ago. Then it pauses at the part when he woke up naked the next morning, yelping at the evidence of his broken condom.

"So, you're... fuck!" Ashton pinches the bridge of his nose before rubbing his face in disbelief. "I knew it. I've seen you before, and you're oddly familiar." He scoots to the closest table and plops down as if he has lost his ability to stand properly.

"Yeah," I reply, almost whispering.

A few minutes pass by in silence; none of us says anything. I know the clock is ticking but I also need to give him time to take this shocking news.

"How long has it been since you found out? Did you know it before you applied for the job in this company?" he asks when he can find his voice again, face facing down at the floor.

"No, I found out after I joined this company. I had a strong suspicion when I saw you for the first time in that Monday meeting. After that, I did my research on your background and my suspicion grew even stronger. Then when I brought Chloe to work, I heard you guys talking about having kids and the party when you broke your condom. It confirmed my theory that you're Chloe's biological father."

He turns his head slightly. "Why didn't you tell me sooner?"

"Fear, I guess, and uncertainty. Look, I know I have a lot of explaining to do. But please, your... Chloe needs you right now."

Still looking baffled, he nods and slowly props himself up. "Alright."

Chapter 16

The trip to the hospital is uncomfortable.

After twenty minutes of talking in private, we went back to his office room and found out the girlfriend was no longer there. Ashton cussed under his breath, but he didn't do anything about her departure. Instead, he grabbed his phone from his upper drawer —that explains why he didn't respond to my call— and slipped it into his pocket before leaving a short message for Andy.

Now here we are, sitting inside his Mercedes-Benz, heading to the hospital. He doesn't want his driver to drive us for some reason, but I'm too scatterbrained to ask at the moment. After giving him the hospital address, I sank myself into the passenger seat and haven't moved a muscle ever since. Luckily, Ashton doesn't seem to be in the mood of talking either.

It's when I realize that my phone is still on silent. I haven't changed it back to ring mode since I left the observation room. Thinking that Sophie might have called me for some important update about Chloe, I retract my phone from my blazer pocket. There is one text from her, saying that Mom and Dad have arrived, and a few missed calls from Ethan.

Ethan. Shit! I totally forgot that I'm supposed to meet him for lunch at the coffee shop. I instantly hit the call button and he picks up on the second ring.

"Char?" Ethan greets, his voice is as calculated as ever.

"Ethan, I'm so, so sorry I stood you up. I completely forgot about our lunch," I squeak.

I can hear him sigh, but it's hard to decide if it's a disappointed sigh. "I was getting worried because you didn't answer my calls. Is everything okay?"

"No." I take a deep breath. Do not cry. Do not cry. Do not cry. "It's Chloe..."

"What about her? Is she alright?"

"No. She's in the hospital now. She got into an accident." Tears are pooling in the corners of my eyes. Damn it. "She's lucky that there are no serious injuries."

"I'm sorry, Char. But I know Chloe is a strong kid," Ethan says. "Is there anything I can do? Should I come to you?"

I shake my head even though I know he can't see me. "No, no need. She's getting the help she needs," I reply, glancing at Ashton who is driving with his gaze fixed on the road. "I'll let you know when she's able to have visitors."

"Okay. Hey, you got this, you hear me? Let me know if you need anything. I mean it, Char. Call me. Anytime."

"Okay. Thank you, Ethan. I'll keep you updated. Bye."

After hanging up the phone call and replying to Sophie's text, I slip my phone back into my pocket and revert my eyes to the road. Another thick silence blankets the air inside my boss's car, but it doesn't bother me a bit. I'm just too exhausted and thirsty. I haven't had anything since my breakfast with Chloe this morning.

"What kind of accident was that?" Ashton's voice pulls me back to the current moment.

"A drunk driver almost hit Chloe's school bus. The bus was trying to avoid it but then it lost control."

"What happened to the drunk driver? Did he escape?"

"No. She hit the tree and died on the spot."

"Good," he mutters under his breath.

"One kid didn't make it, though." I whimper as I rub my forehead. "It was so heartbreaking and terrifying. What if it was Chloe? I just can't lose her."

Tears escape my eyes again. I turn my head to the passenger's window, not wanting him to see me crying. I just can't help myself from being an emotional wreck right now. Ashton says nothing but he reaches out to give my shoulder a soft squeeze, and it's enough for me. Having emotional support from Chloe's father, regardless of how weird our situation is, makes me feel somehow braver.

"Thank you for doing this. For Chloe," I mumble as I grab a pack of tissue from my bag to blow my nose.

"Don't mention it. I will do it for her even if we're not related." Ashton taps his finger against the steering wheels, his face frowning. "You said they don't have enough supply for her blood type. What kind of hospital is that?" A grim coats Ashton's voice.

"It's a small hospital in town, just the closest they can get for the emergency, I guess." I shrug. "They said they are calling around now, but they don't know how fast the supply arrives. Meanwhile, if someone can give direct transfusion, it would cut off the waiting time."

"After she's released from the ER, you should transfer her to a better hospital. My family doctor will take care of the transfer."

"Please, sir. Let's just focus on what we're doing now," I reply, feeling annoyed all of a sudden. I know he means well, but his impulse to take control of everything pokes my nerves.

"Alright. And call me Ashton when we're not at work."

"Okay."

"And I want to take a DNA test."

Of course he's going to ask for this, and I'm not against it at all. He has a right to demand one after I dropped the bomb. "Sure."

"Right now, it's still hard for me to stomach this information." We stop at a traffic light, and he uses the chance to give me his full attention. "It's not that I don't believe you. I do. And I'm not blind to see our resemblance. But I need to have proper evidence that Chloe really is my daughter, for a legal purpose."

"You don't have to explain. I understand completely."

As the car is moving again, I glance at the outside mirror, looking at my reflection. A miserable woman with a pallid face and swollen eyes is staring back at me. I can't remember when was the last time I cried this hard. Probably it was when I learned that Ethan left for good.

"You should close your eyes and rest a bit. We still have fifteen minutes until we reach the hospital."

Mom and Sophie are sitting at the far corner of the ER waiting room, while Dad is nowhere in sight. He's probably getting Diana from school. Once I reach them, Mom pulls me into her warm embrace.

"She survived the accident. She's such a strong girl," she croaks. Judging from her throaty voice, she must have cried for some time.

I nod quietly against her hair because I'm afraid if I open my mouth, I will be breaking into tears again. It's when I see Sophie freeze on her seat, gaping in the direction behind me.

At the same time, I hear my mom shriek, "Oh my god. Isn't he..."

When I pull out from Mom, the two ladies are gawking at Ashton as if they are looking at Saint Claus in summer. I know they noticed who he is at once. Chloe's biological father.

I clear my throat. "Mom, Soph, this is Mist...Ashton, um, he's going to help out with the direct blood transfusion," I say, deliberately skipping the 'he's Chloe's dad' part since there is no official evidence just yet. I turn my head to Ashton. "These are my mom, Sofia, and my sister, Sophie."

"Mmm, about that," Sophie murmurs, biting her lower lip and glancing at me and Ashton, "we just got notified that the blood supply for Chloe has arrived. They are now waiting for you to sign the consent form."

"Oh." I blink.

So, the blood supply for Chloe is here, while the living source of supply is standing behind me, for nothing. I should have known that the hospital would get it faster from the bank donor instead of dragging Chloe's father here. At least it would have saved my energy from dealing with the Ashton Knight.

"That's very good news," says a deep voice behind me before his hand gives me a gentle push on my lower back. "Let's go." Of course. He will have this urge to push people forward, figuratively and literally, even when he knows damn well that he isn't in charge of this situation.

Before I sign the form, the doctor informs us of the pros and cons of the blood transfusion, along with the risks that might follow. Ashton can't have a say or decide anything since he's practically not a family member, but I can see how his lips twitch and how restless he becomes during the process. Thank god he knows what he needs to do, which is shut his mouth.

As soon as the blood transfusion is done, Chloe is ready to be transferred to a patient room. Mom and Sophie leave for their late lunch at the hospital cafeteria while I stay put in the waiting room. Ashton decides to go with them to grab something for me to eat, which makes me wonder if I dragged the same Ashton as the one I knew last month.

I've been thinking about his idea of moving Chloe to a better hospital, but then it will be farther from home. I'm not sure if it's practical for all of us. Despite not being awake yet, Chloe's condition is progressing well. Maybe I should see first what happens in the next twenty-four hours before making the important decision.

My train of thought is disrupted when someone nudges my shoulder as he plops down on the seat beside me. I don't have to look to find out because his scent is enough to announce his presence, though I've noticed that he smells slightly different, probably because of all this rush and stress in the past few hours. But I find it more masculine, especially since it's mixed with a pinch of woody notes of his perfumes. I breathe in his scent secretly, even though it's not helping me get over his effect on me. But to my defense, I'm defenseless today.

"Try to eat something." He hands me a salmon sandwich.

"Thanks," I mumble as I open the plastic wrap.

After making sure I eat, he unwraps his bread roll and silently takes a bite before scrunching his nose. "Hospital food sucks."

I can't help chuckling at his remark. "Better than an empty tummy," I say, earning a shrug from him.

"That is true," he says. "I can't stay long though. I need to go back soon."

I nod. "Thank you for staying, and I'm sorry for what happened between you and your girlfriend."

"Girlfriend?" He raises an eyebrow. "Oh, you mean Diandra."

"Isn't she your girlfriend?"

Ashton purses his lips before taking another bite. "It's complicated," he answers after he swallows.

Of course he will pick a vague answer. He's not the kind who talks about his personal life after all. "Well, anyway, sorry for creating the drama between you two. And knowing that it could've been avoided, now I do feel bad."

"It could've been avoided?"

"Well, apparently, Chloe got the supply before we arrived here. So, I could have just waited here and saved us all the office drama."

"And continue to keep me in the dark?" A deep frown is forming on Ashton's face. "You should have told me this months ago, Charlotte, not waited until she needed something from me. I have to say, I'm not very happy with this situation."

I gulp. "Right. I'm sorry about that." I wish I had the energy to have a real talk with him, but right now, I'm so close to crumbling down. "I owe you an explanation. I will tell you everything when Chloe is in the clear. I promise."

He fixes his gaze on me for a few seconds longer than needed. "I'm holding you to it."

Chapter 17

It has been twenty-four hours since Chloe received the blood transfusion, and there have been no signs of acute reactions. She was awake last night, just to groan and lazily sweep the room with her green eyes before her gaze stopped at my face. I rushed to sit next to her and held her hand, the one which wasn't wrapped in gypsum. Not long after that, her eyelids began to drop again. She had a mild fever after midnight, but the nurse said it was a common reaction and it would resolve by itself, and it did.

Chloe is doing much better today. She's longer awake, more responsive, and begins to take her fluid orally. Even though the time goes excruciatingly slow at the moment, I won't dare to push my luck. Her steady progress is all I ask for, and it becomes my strength to go through the day.

Sitting on Chloe's balcony, mom and I spend our late afternoon drinking tea while keeping an eye on Chloe and Diana conversing inside the hospital room. My daughter's plump lips curl up into a weak smile now and then as her eyes beam at her cousin's blabber.

"Have you heard from her father?" asks Mom, half whispering so that the kids can't hear us through the slightly open door. Ever since she met Chloe's biological father, I can tell that she's been dying to learn more about him. It's a good thing that my mom is way less impulsive than I am.

"No." I shake my head. "I promised I would let him know when there was a drastic change in her condition."

"Well, she's awake and the transfusion went well. Isn't it drastic enough?"

"What I mean by drastic is if her condition is dropping, or when she's discharged from the hospital. You know what I mean." I chew my bottom lip, starting to doubt my own answer. "I mean, he's a busy man, I don't need to report to him every hour."

"Hmm. I think he would appreciate it nonetheless. She's his daughter after all."

"I just told him about his daughter yesterday, Mom. I don't think he has the 'I am the daddy' mentality yet. Also, if he really is curious about Chl... her progress, he could have called me and asked, but he didn't." Glancing at the kids who are now savoring every page of the latest pre-teenage magazine, I grab the bottled water from the small table that separates us. I take a few sips from it. "I believe he just needs time to process it. He got bombarded by wild facts that will change his life forever. I'm going to let him deal with it at his own pace. He knows where to find us when he's ready."

"He didn't seem to have trouble accepting the fact that he was her dad." Mom lowers her tone, almost whispering.

"I wouldn't say that. He had a hard time taking this but he was good at hiding it. It's a skill required in his job: poker face."

"He was pretty concerned about you two yesterday. He even came to the cafeteria to make sure you had something to eat." A faint smirk grows in the corner of her lips.

I scoff, knowing where Mom is getting at. Gosh, how can this man charm people around him so effortlessly? "No, you're wrong there. He has a girlfriend, kinda." As I say it, the image of the red-haired woman pops up in my head, followed by jealousy creeping in.

No, I can't have feelings for him because he's Chloe's dad. Messing around with a random hot guy is a thing, but not if it risks my job, and more to it, if it affects Chloe. Between Ashton and I, it will be strictly about co-parenting, if he wants to be in Chloe's life. I can't add more drama to it.

"Oh? I wonder how his girlfriend will take this."

I shrug. "I don't know, and I don't care."

Mom keeps her gaze on me for a few more seconds and I hate it when she does that. It feels like she can see right through me. I'm just so naked and defenseless under her scrutinizing eyes.

"How are you going to break this news to Chloe?" When she realizes she mentions the name by accident she bites her lip while quickly glancing at the pair. Luckily, the two girls are oblivious.

"Don't know. First, we're going to wait for the DNA result, then we see where we go from there."

"Fair enough, even though anyone with eyes can see that she is his kid," Mom mumbles. "Give him an update. Maybe he's just clueless about how to be a father all of a sudden, but here is your part to help him. For your daughter's sake."

Mom's words bug me for the rest of the day. Maybe she's right about it. Maybe Ashton is just clueless and doesn't know how to handle this situation. Sending him a small update about Chloe doesn't hurt anyone, does it?

Me: The blood transfusion went well. And she is awake.

After two minutes of waiting and still not getting a response, I slip my phone back into my bag and head to the family room where patients can meet their visitors outside their rooms. It's also where other parents spend their evening until bedtime. Right now, talking with people over coffee sounds more appealing than watching Chloe asleep while pondering about her dad.

What do I expect? Of course, he doesn't check his phone. He's probably with Diandra now, in a romantic candlelight dinner, fixing the damage I created.

It's past breakfast time when I'm busy replying to emails from work, with Chloe's soft snoring in the background. Despite progressing well, she still dozes off a lot due to the painkiller for her healing wound. She's also forced to stay put in bed because she can't walk yet, which makes her fall asleep more often out of boredom.

Ashton replied to my text message two nights ago with a simple "that's good", and I hit a road end, clueless about what I should do afterward. But since I had to focus on my daughter's recovery, I've decided to let him be. I stand corrected in my opinion that he knows when to find us when he's ready.

Apparently, this is the day. When I'm about to click the 'Send' button on my email for my client, my phone vibrates.

Knight, Asston: Can I see her?

In the next second, another message comes through.

Ethan: Hey, how are you holding up and how is your little girl doing? Is she allowed to have a visitor yet?

How did the messages from Chloe's ghost daddy and living daddy arrive at the same time? Smiling, I reply to them with the same message: Chloe's room number, and the visiting hours, hoping that they won't show up on the same day and at the same time.

But of course, they do.

On the next day, the two men show up at Chloe's door, wearing the same color suits, with identical balloons in their hands. Sandy, who is also visiting Chloe, almost chokes on her drink at the view.

The four of us stare at each other for a few seconds until Chloe squeals, "Are those for me?" Her eyes are twinkling at the pink get-well-soon balloons in Pony shape.

"Yes," Ashton and Ethan reply in unison before glaring at each other.

I quickly stand up with the huge grin I can muster, "Do come in and have a seat! What a nice surprise to see you both visit Chloe," I say cheerfully as I take the balloons from them. Groaning under my breath, I tie up the ropes to the hospital bed frame.

Sandy gets up and greets everyone before arranging two seats next to Chloe's bed. And such a good friend she is, she then scoots over to the other side of the bed, making sure she gets the best spot to enjoy the show.

"So, how is my little girl doing? I heard she survived the big crash boom bang last Monday," Ethan starts.

"Yes, I heard the bang! But I didn't see what happened, because I was already here when I woke up." Chloe smiles from ear to ear before glancing at Ashton and sheepishly greeting, "Hello, sir boss."

"Uh, Chloe," I interrupt. "You can just call him sir, or Mr. Knight."

"Call me Ashton," Ashton corrects me.

Chloe's eyes widen. "But you're Mama's big big boss!"

"Yeah, and?"

"I can get Mama in trouble if I'm not polite to her bosses," Chloe says, half whispering at Ashton. I still have no clue where she got this idea. She never gave me clear answers to it.

"Well, right now I'm not her boss. We are not at the office, right?"

Chloe tilts her head. "So, are you here because you're Mama's friend now?"

Ashton nods. "Something like that, and your friend, too, of course," he replies, earning a frown from Ethan.

"Ah, okay. I do call Mama's friends by their first name, except Nolan." Chloe looks at Ethan as she smiles brightly at him.

Ashton raises his eyebrow, looking intrigued. "Oh, why is that?"

"Because I don't like his first name."

Oh boy.

"Why not?"

"He has the same name as my father's." The smile disappears from Chloe's face.

"Chloe, sweetie, you haven't drunk enough since you woke up. Why don't you drink a bit?" I interject, then nervously turn my head to the two men. "And I'm going to grab some coffee. Anyone wants some?"

Every pair of eyes is on me, except Ashton's.

"And may I know what your father's name is?"

"Ethan. Ethan Watkins."

Chapter 18

After having a Chinese take-out, Ethan and I head to the family room to let Chloe have her night sleep. Ashton left a couple of hours ago for a dinner appointment, but despite his brief visit to see Chloe, it brings a new hope that he may have started to come to terms with having a daughter.

"He's Chloe's father, isn't he?" Ethan asks, his eyes fixed on the coffee vending machine that is now making a fluttering noise.

"Yeah." I nod. "Obvious, isn't it?"

"And Chloe still thinks I'm her biological father."

"Ethan Watkins. Not you. You are Ethan Nolan for her."

Ethan shoots me a glare. "Char, I am Ethan Watkins. Sooner or later she's going to find out. Once she discovers the magic of the Google search engine, she will learn that my name is Ethan Watkins."

"Okay, okay. I know I need to fix this soon," I mumble as I cross one arm over my chest while my other hand massages my temple. "Just give me a couple of weeks tops. I want Chloe to be at least a bit stronger to take all of this information. But I promise I'll sort this out."

"This is so messed up, you know. She despises Ethan Watkins, which is me, but also not me. On the other hand, you let her believe that Ashton Knight is a friend while he's the one who is responsible for this mess."

"No," I interject. "If anything, I'm the one who is responsible for this. I'm the one who lied. Ashton didn't know about Chloe until last Monday."

Ethan frowns as he stares blankly at the machine in front of him, seeming busy with his thoughts. I don't know what's on his mind right now, but I can't let him blame Ashton for the mess I created.

As soon as the black liquid stops flowing, he picks up the cup and hands it to me before setting up another cup on the machine tray. "Are you and Ashton...a thing?"

I stop sipping on my coffee, my lips hovering over its cup rim. "Huh? How did you get the idea?"

"You should answer a question with an answer, Char, not with another question. I'm not your client."

"I thought it was more a lawyer thing." I shrug.

"Touche." Ethan chuckles as he slips his hands into his pockets, staring back at the machine that is making the same noise once again. "But seriously, though. Are you guys maybe looking into some kind of relationship in regards to raising Chloe together?"

I shake my head. "No. It's been only a working relationship between me and Ashton. And I want to keep it that way when we start with the co-parenting role. Second of all, he has someone."

"Hmm, okay." I can almost hear the relieved tone in his voice. "Then I read it wrong."

I tilt my head, feeling anxious all of sudden. "What do you mean?"

"Nothing. It's just...the way you looked at him while he and Chloe were talking made me feel...left out." Ethan almost mumbles when he says the last word.

His somber expression tugs at my heartstring. He's been going through dark moments, and seeing him like this makes me sad for him. "I wasn't trying to make anyone feel left out. I was just glad that Chloe has a chance to connect with her father after everything she's been through. But that's all about it."

He turns his head to me, his dark eyes glinting under the dim light. "That's all about it?"

"Yeah," I reply, ignoring the uneasiness that is creeping up inside me.

Ethan's lips curl up into a smile. "That's the answer I expected to hear from you, to be honest."

"Oh?"

"Char, I've been–"

"Excuse me," says a voice behind us, startling us. "Are you two done with the vending machine?"

"Oh, yes. My apology for standing in the way," Ethan replies as he snatches his cup from the machine. Once we find a table in the corner of the room, he continues, "I believe you've noticed by now, that I want us to try again."

"Ethan–" I'm about to say something but Ethan raises his hand to stop me.

"Let me finish first. I know I messed up big time back then. I didn't trust you enough and chose to believe other people over my own girlfriend. I had no idea that Lydia stirred this problem just to break us up."

Ethan mentioning the girl's name brings up my old resentment to the surface. I always knew that behind her friendly smile, Lydia had been wanting him for herself but he was just too stubborn to see it. Ethan took her words seriously because they'd been buddies for years before I came into his life, and she knew it damn well.

"And it was too late when I realized it. Three months late, and you were already carrying someone's baby. It crushed me big time. I know you said you still wanted us and after the delivery, you wanted to try again. But the pregnancy messed up my head. And I ran away." Ethan sighs in exasperation. "That was the biggest mistake I made, Char. Because no matter where I went, no matter what I did, you're always there in the back of my mind."

"Yet you never tried to find me," I mutter under my breath.

"I know. I've been denying my feelings for years. I thought by carrying on with my life, focusing on my career, meeting someone new, falling in love again, and having a kid would just get my life back in gear." Ethan takes a gulp of his coffee as if it will give him the courage to what he's going to say next. "But once I saw you again that day, I knew I'd been fooling myself all these years. I still love you, Char. I've always loved you. It's been eight years and nothing has changed."

I open my mouth before closing it again. I've been waiting for this moment forever; the moment Ethan finally admits that he made a mistake by leaving me. There are so many things I want to throw at his face right now. I want to tell him about how much he hurt me, how much he broke me, and how I became dysfunctional in a long-term relationship ever since.

The thing is that even though my mind is now running a mile, my heart refuses to budge. Because I can't hate him. Maybe I have forgiven him at some point in my life without realizing it. I can't hold his mistake against him forever, can I? If I heard that he impregnated a random girl right after we broke up that day, I would be as devastated as he was. Hell, I would probably do worse things than just disappearing on him.

But the question is: do I want to reopen the door for him? Do I still want us?

"I know the timing is just not in our favor. We both are still in the mess, but I don't mind waiting." Ethan runs his fingers through his black hair as he smiles weakly. "Honestly, I didn't plan to say this to you today. I guess, learning about Chloe meeting her dad pokes my nerves. The thought of losing you once again scares me."

"I don't know what to say. I'm just...my brain is just not functioning at the moment," I say.

"That's why I said I would wait. Take as much time as you need. I'm not going anywhere this time, Char."

I shift my gaze to him and our eyes meet. Unlike eight years ago, I see no doubt coating his dark eyes. The man who is now sitting in front of me is the Ethan I wished he had been back then. Maybe, just maybe, I can still find my way back to him.

Fumbling with my empty paper cup, I smile and nod. "Okay."

Chloe has been a fighter since the very beginning of her existence.

She is getting stronger and has started to stand up and walk. Just a few steps at a time until she can reach the bathroom and say goodbye to the urine pot she's grown to despise. It's been a week since the accident and judging from Chloe's recovery progress, I can go back to work today. I'm so grateful to have Mom and Sophie who are willing to take a turn in keeping an eye on Chloe while I'm away. And the good news is, she's expected to be discharged sometime this week.

Max agreed to my proposal in taking a half-day of work until Chloe is settled at home. I just need to pop up at work to sort out things I can not do from home, such as client visits and some paperwork. My team has been nothing but supportive. Even the sassy Gina keeps making sure that I'm holding on just fine with the workload.

It's almost lunch break when my intercom rings. I'm in the middle of rechecking my to-do list for tomorrow before I can pack my bag and head to the cafeteria, my last stop before I go to see Chloe. At this point, I would do anything to avoid the hospital cafeteria. Ashton is right about the food. It sucks.

"Hello, Charlotte speaking," I greet as I press the phone receiver between my ear and my shoulder, my hands busy throwing all my stationery into the drawer.

"Come to my office. I've ordered lunch for us and it's time to have a little talk."

I freeze. That voice.

The last encounter we had in the hospital is still left un-solved. Ashton hasn't pursued further explanation about how Chloe's father is Ethan Watkins. I did tell him briefly that it was some kind of misinformation and I would explain more later. He just nodded and said "okay" before he left the hospital.

And now he wants what is promised to him.

Chapter 19

Standing in front of this wooden door again feels like a Déjà vu. Only, the executive assistant's desk is now occupied by a frowning secretary who gives me a pitying look. Not wanting to give him the idea why I'm here, I just shrug at Andy. If he thinks that I'm in some kind of trouble, then he's not wrong.

Two knocks and the door is pulled open, revealing our CEO who summoned me to his chamber. If I didn't know that there was a camera above my head, I would've been swooned by the thought that he must have been standing behind the door for a good ten minutes, waiting for my arrival. But now I know better.

I smile at him brightly. "Sir."

"Miss Garnett, please, come in." He moves to the side while holding the door open for me.

Once inside, my eyes catch a huge food platter sitting on his coffee table. My mouth waters instantly when I see the mixed sushi rolls, which are enough to feed the whole floor, are arranged in a zig-zag around three small sauce bowls. Coming up here isn't a bad idea after all.

Wait, or is it some kind of a trap?

The clicking sound of the door lock prompts me to stop short and slowly turn around. He never locked the door when he had company before.

Ashton smiles at me, rather eerily. "What are you waiting for?" he says. "Go ahead, eat as much as your stomach can handle. I know you're on the verge of killing yourself because of that hospital food."

I walk to the sofa while eyeing the luxurious lunch my not-so-generous boss has prepared for me. He can't be this nice, can he? What is he up to? Does he want to gain something in return; something I might not like?

"Charlotte." Ashton sighs. "We don't have much time. Go dive in and don't worry, the food isn't...overly spiced up."

Ignoring the dangerous subject he tried to poke, I nod as I grab the small plate and a pair of chopsticks. For now, I will not dwell on my suspicions because what I need is a clear mind for the talk, and I won't get to that state with a growling tummy.

Ashton takes the reading chair across the table, facing me. Crossing his legs, he places both his hands on the armrests. He taps his fingers mindlessly while his emerald green eyes never leave me as I try to enjoy my food.

Feeling the growing discomfort of being watched while eating, I tilt my head to him. "Don't you need to eat, too?"

Ashton brings his hands together, interlaces his fingers, and rests his chin on top of them. He slowly shakes his head. "I'm still full. I had a brunch meeting a couple of hours ago."

"Alright," I mumble as I fill my plate with the next batch of sushi rolls. If he wants to just sit there and watch me eat, then I won't let him stop me from savoring the free food. I know he's not lying when he says he's still full. During the time I was working as his assistant, he would only have his coffee for lunch when he had a brunch meeting.

"That guy in the hospital isn't Ethan Nolan. He is Ethan Watkins," he starts after I finish my third plate. "So, how did he become Chloe's father now?"

I knew he would start the investigation once he left the hospital. If he could figure out the chili sauce prank in one night, he must have had all the information he needs about Ethan by now.

"It's a long story, but I'm going to fix it," I answer quickly.

"That's not an answer to my question, Charlotte."

Resting my plate on my lap, I take a few sips of bottled water. "Chloe kept asking me who his father was and why he wasn't around. I just couldn't tell her that she was conceived in a one-night stand, and that I didn't know who her father was. She was only four. So, I lied. I told her that her father was my college sweetheart who left me after a disagreement. When I found out I was pregnant, he was already out of the radar."

"It doesn't explain the Ethan Watkins part," Ashton says.

"I'm getting to that part. So, I was caught up in the circle of lies about Chloe's father. When she grew bigger and asked me the same question again —she asked about her father's name this time, I still couldn't bring myself to tell her the truth. And I told her her father was Ethan Watkins."

"Ethan was your boyfriend, wasn't he?"

Avoiding his boring eyes, I nod while staring at my plate. "I picked answers that's closest to the truth, just to make the deception less deceiving, you know." When I see the frown on his face, I wave my hand in a dismissive gesture. "Never mind. It's stupid."

"No. Tell me everything."

I sigh, feeling my head become heavy. "Around the time I was pregnant with Chloe, Ethan did leave me. So, I didn't lie about that part. I just left the tiny bit of details that he was not the one who got me pregnant." I wince when I say my last line.

The frown on his face gets deeper every second. His lips twitch but he doesn't interrupt my explanation.

"Basically, I just borrowed my ex's name until I can come up with the truth when she's older. Little did I know that he showed up at a not very favorable time."

Ashton squints his eyes at me. "So, Watkins left because you were pregnant with Chloe?"

"Yeah."

It takes him almost thirty seconds before he carefully asks, "Are you two...getting back together?"

I bite my inner cheek, wondering about these two men asking the same darn question. "I don't think this is relevant to our topic."

Ashton raises one eyebrow. "It is. I'd like to know who is in Chloe's life if I'm going to bond with her."

"Why?"

"I want to know if she has another father figure at the moment, considering she hates her biological father. I need to see what I can do and what I can't do."

I purse my lips, deciding how far I'm going to tell him about me and Ethan. "It's always been just me and Chloe. Men came and went but I never let them get too close to Chloe."

"I disagree. Watkins seems close with Chloe." If a tone could cut, the sushi in front of us would've been in a million pieces by now.

"Ethan adores Chloe, true, but he's not trying to fill in a father figure or anything." It's quite the opposite if I may add, but I keep the last part to myself.

The scowl is growing more prominent on Ashton's face. "And he doesn't mind about his name being borrowed?"

"Of course he does. I know this is such a mess. I'm going to fix this. I promise."

Silence permeates the air between us. Ashton seems to take his time processing the information I just told him. Not wanting to intrude on his train of thought, I revert my attention to the sushi and carefully pick up the salmon nigiri with my chopsticks. As the mix of the soft salmon, the rice, the ginger, and the sauce melts on my tongue, a moan escapes my lips.

"Please, can you not make that sound? It's distracting."

"Sorry," I reply quickly, adjusting my posture and sitting straight before resuming eating. I just can't get enough of this. The caterer must be the one from the day I brought Chloe to work. I'm in the middle of contemplating asking him if I can bring the rest home when I hear his deep voice again.

"So, Chloe hates me."

"No. She hates the character I made up. And I'm going to make this right once the DNA result is out."

"About that, I want to do it this week, if you don't mind. My family doctor will take care of this. He will be contacting you about the details."

"Sure. No problem."

"Once it's proven that she is mine, we will be having more discussion about how we're going to do this. The serious one."

"I wouldn't expect any less than that, sir," I reply as I nod. I know it's going to be a long journey from that point onward. But I'm ready for it. For Chloe.

The DNA result has come back and it confirmed that Ashton Knight is Chloe's biological father. I'm not surprised, yet knowing that Chloe now officially found her daddy makes me feel sentimental in a way.

Ashton is no different. The first thing he manages to say when he gets a hold of me is "I'm her dad. I'm Chloe's father" with an amount of emotion I've never heard from him before.

I know he's been trying to deal with the possible reality that he has a kid, something he never planned to have, but when the test result confirmed it, it has become real now.

"I know this isn't easy for you," I say, thinking back about the day I found out I was pregnant with Chloe. "I've been there, and trust me, it will get easier. Take your time and let this sink in first. Meanwhile, I'm going to fix the mess I made. I need to talk to her about who her dad is."

"Okay, thanks."

I sigh, feeling my stomach churn. "She might take this badly though. Maybe she's going to hate me once she learns I've been lying to her."

"Do you need me to be there when you do it?"

"No. It's between me and her. Thanks for the offer," I mumble, glancing at the time on my GPS screen. I'm on my way home, but I had to pull over to pick up his call. "I need to hang up now or I will be late getting her from Sophie's house."

Chloe has been home for almost a week now. She's getting stronger and more mobile every day, but she still needs to wait for school. Since I need to start working full-time again, I drop her off every morning at Sophie's house if it's not Mom's turn to watch over her.

After picking her up, we head home and start with dinner. By 7 PM, we're done with our evening meal, and I let Chloe watch TV while I clean up. She helps me with the dishes on normal days, even though I hardly call it help. She tends to rearrange everything I've put in the dishwasher. It bugs her when things aren't put in their proper group of cooking and eating utensils.

When I join her in the living room, Chloe is busy drawing an astronaut on her gypsum that is almost full of her gravity work. She will miss it when they take it off next week. I plop down next to her and take the remote control from the table.

"Why did you turn it off?" she protests when I press the power button. "It's not bedtime yet."

"No, it's not. But I need to talk to you."

"About what? Is it about Mr. and Mrs. Donegal? I haven't spied on them again, Mama."

"No, it's not about Mr. and Mrs. Donegal. It's about your father."

Chapter 20

Chloe stares at me, a mix of curiosity and resentment flashing in her emerald green eyes. She then mumbles, "Okay." With that, she puts back on the lid of the marker in her hand and neatly places it on the coffee table.

I wait until she snuggles comfortably next to me. "Can I ask again why you hate Ethan Watkins?"

"You know why. It's because he left you and that is mean," she answers in a hardened tone. She's been giving me the same answer every time I asked this, but deep down I know she resents the father figure because of his absence in her life.

"Umm. Well..." I clear my throat before continuing, "Adult people have arguments. Sometimes, they can't find a common ground and decide to take separate ways, so that they don't have to keep fighting and be sad all the time."

"But he left when you still loved him, Mama."

I wince inwardly. When Chloe asked this question for the first time, I still held the tiny bit of hope that Ethan would come back to find me. Just as Taylor Dayne said in her song, Love Will Lead You Back. But after five years, I started to accept that the song wasn't for me.

"Yeah, but that was not the only reason he left." When Chloe looks up at me with a confused look, I add, "I also made a mistake that pushed him away."

"What mistake?"

I bite my lower lip, thinking about what kind of answer I will give her. What mistake exactly? Was sleeping with someone else after getting ditched by my boyfriend a mistake? Was the decision to carry on with the pregnancy a mistake?

"Well, for me, it wasn't a mistake. But he saw it as one back in the day." I click my tongue as an idea flashes in my mind. "Something like when we do the dishwashing together. I don't find throwing everything into the dishwasher not in a proper order a problem, but it always bugs you. Imagine if I never listened to you or let you rearrange them, what would you do?"

Chloe purses her lips and shrugs. "Then I don't want to help anymore, and just go see my cartoon."

"Exactly. You would leave because you can't stand the way I do the dishwashing."

Chloe frowns, looking deep into her own thoughts. "But I don't go and leave the house and never come back, I just go to see my cartoon."

"Well, it's just a small example, but what Ethan Watkins and I had was more than just a dishwashing problem, sweetie. It was uh... adult stuff that gave lots of headaches."

"Still, if he loved you he wouldn't leave. Just as you said all the time, no matter how naughty I am, you will never leave me, because you love me."

Chloe is probably right about Ethan shouldn't having left me if he loved me, but the comparison she's making isn't apple to apple. What I have for her is nothing like what he had for me for sure.

"First of all, when a boy and a girl fall in love, they can fall out of love and then break up. But mother's love doesn't work that way." I smile at her before giving her a peck on the forehead. "Mama will never fall out of love with you. Ever."

Chloe's lips curl into a smile as her eyes twinkle. "Okay."

"Second of all," I say as I take a deep breath, "I have a confession to make."

My daughter's head snaps in my direction. "What did you do? Were you being naughty?" she asks, repeating the same exact line I gave her every time she said she had a confession to make.

"Yes. Very naughty," I reply. "I... lied to you... about who your father is." When the smile on Chloe's face falters and confusion takes over, I close my eyes. I need to do it now or never. "Ethan Watkins is not your father."

Chloe freezes. I count every second that passes, and she starts shifting on her spot at the twelfth second. "He is not?"

I open my eyes and her pellucid green eyes lock with mine. "No."

"Who then?"

"Your father is Ashton Knight."

Chloe gasps. "Do you mean your big big boss?"

I nod as I swallow the imaginary lump in my throat. "He's the one, yeah. But, everything I told you about Ethan Watkins is true, except for you are not his baby. We broke up, and then I met your dad briefly. In the next three months, I found out that you were already snuggling in Mama's tummy."

Chloe frowns at my explanation, probably trying to catch up with every single word that just rolled off my tongue at high speed, the thing I do when I'm caught lying. "Where was Mr. Knight when I was in your tummy?"

"Honestly? I didn't know where he was. We spent a very brief moment together and didn't plan to continue the...uh, the thing we had. We had no idea that I fell pregnant later on. We had different schools, different jobs, different lives, and we never bumped into each other again until recently."

I study her face intently as she stares blankly at our coffee table. I would give anything to know what's going on inside her head right now.

"Did you love Mr. Knight then? Did you love my father?" she asks, catching me off guard.

"Uh, no, not really. We didn't know each other back then. Why did you ask?"

"Baby is made out of love." Her face grows darker, a sign that she's not happy. "Was I a mistake baby, Mama?"

"No, no, no, no, no," I slide off the sofa and down on my knees so that I can look her in the eye. "You. Were. Never. A. Mistake. For. Me. Also not for your father. Never were and never will be." The prominent frown on her face shoots a panic twist in my stomach. "Okay, I'll make another confession to make, but this is just between us, okay?"

My daughter tilts her head before nodding hesitantly.

"I was attracted to your father. To me, he was a super cool guy with a pair of emerald green eyes" —I touch her eyelid lightly— "and brown hair." I caress her hair lightly, earning me a faint smile from my little one. "You see, the seed of love was already there. Sadly, we didn't see each other long enough to grow it into a tree of love. I'm sure we would have fallen madly in love with each other if we were given a chance."

My explanation seems to soothe my daughter. The scowl begins to leave her face, but I can tell that her mind is still busy processing.

"If Mr. Knight is my father, do I have to stay with him every weekend?"

I raise my eyebrow at her question. "If you want to. And if he's free. The question is, do you want to?"

Chloe shakes her head. "No. But Marisa has to stay with her dad every weekend, even when she doesn't want to."

I chuckle softly. "Every parent has their own rules, sweetie. Marisa stays with her dad on weekends because her mom and dad agree to the arrangement, and they see that it's important for Marisa to spend time with her dad." I rub her legs softly. "But you, little Missy, don't have to do something you don't want to, for now. Okay?"

Chloe nods, but from the glint in her eyes, she is still not done with all the questions about her newfound father. And I can't blame her. She deserves all the time she needs to come to terms that her father is the green-eyed stranger from Mama's work, not the meanie Ethan Watkins--

"And oh, I have another confession."

Chloe's eyes widen. "Do I have one more father?"

"No," I reply quickly. "It's about Nolan. His name is not Ethan Nolan. He is Ethan Watkins." Looking at Chloe's confused expression, I slightly regret bringing this up right now. I should have waited for this and let Chloe settle first with the daddy story. "Mama was afraid that you would think he was your father when you met him at Maura's cafe. So, I lied, again."

"You lied a lot, Mama."

"I know." I bury my face against her tummy and mumble, "I'm so, so, so, sorry. This is a very bad example for you. Lying is bad. And Mama feels so bad now."

I feel her hand on my hair. "We are only humans. We make mistakes," she mutters, repeating the exact line Sophie says from time to time when one of us makes a stupid mistake, but not this kind of mistake. I wonder if Chloe understands the weight of the lines she just said. Nevertheless, it gives me hope that one day, she will forgive me completely.

"Thank you, sweetie. I will be honest from now on, okay?"

"Promise?"

"Promise."

I rest my head on her tights, letting my nose snuggle on her protruding belly, inhaling her in. I close my eyes when her little fingers run through my hair. For the first time in the past four years, the lingering heaviness from my chest is being lifted. I'm freed from the circle of lies I've been building around me and my daughter.

Chapter 21

Chloe has been having a hard time accepting the new fact about her father.

She's turned noticeably quiet, spaces out a lot, and changes the subject every time I bring up Ashton Knight's name. My daughter is introverted despite her straightforward nature. For something that she's still unsure about, she tends to keep it to herself even though the never-ending frown on her face gives away enough. And that is what's happening right now.

When I confide in my sister, Sophie believes it's just a phase and I should give Chloe some more time.

"She's been holding this resentment toward her father when she still thought it was Ethan Watkins. I think she's still trying to address her own feelings about this daddy stuff," she says. "You should let her deal with this at her own pace."

I bite my lower lip as I turn my head to check on Chloe and Diana. The pair is now busy making a necklace out of string and beads in the living room, pre-teen movie is playing in the background. I'm glad that my sister came to bring Diana to spend Sunday afternoon with Chloe since she still refuses to see Ashton.

Despite the cool breeze from the spring weather, Sophie and I are sitting on my balcony, curling up under the blanket on the hanging bench while having a sister-to-sister talk.

"I feel like I'm the shittiest mother on earth, you know," I mumble in defeat.

"How so?"

"I've been lying to her a lot. I let her live under the impression that her father is doing something bad to me while I know she's longing for a father figure." My hand clutches the blanket harder and presses it into my chest, shuddering at the thought. "What was I thinking?"

Sophie sits closer to me and wraps her hand around my shoulders, pulling me to her. "That's not true. I saw it myself that you kept correcting her from having the idea that her father was a bad guy. You kept emphasizing that having a disagreement is a normal thing for a couple."

"And it didn't work. Didn't you see how spiteful she was that day when she thought Ethan was her father?"

Sophie sighs, staring blankly at the oak tree in my backyard while her hand is playing with my hair. "Honestly, I think it happens to most kids. When their parents split up on bad terms, they're kinda forced to choose. You did what you could do, Char."

"I don't know about that. It feels like I could've done better than just lying to her face."

"Yeah. Lying about her father's identity was not a smart move. And now it's kinda messed up." Sophie tries to smile emphatically but it looks more like a wince. "How did Ashton take her refusal?"

I shrug. "If he was disappointed, he didn't say it. It's not like I could see his face. We only talk through texts."

"How are you guys going to do this by the way? I mean, seeing you two are working in the same office, are you going to announce that your daughter is also your CEO's?"

"No. Hell, no. The last thing I want them to know is Ashton's connection to me outside work life. I'm still on my probation now. People are still watching me like a hawk to see if I'm capable of this job. If they knew about Chloe, they would think I got the job because of Ashton."

"What did he say about this?"

"He agreed and understands my points. Besides, what we are focusing on now is how to make Chloe warm up to him."

Sophie nods. "Chloe just needs time to process, trust me. She's a smart kid. First, she needs to unravel her resentment towards Ethan Watkins which has no base anymore. I mean, maybe she will still dislike Ethan Watkins as your ex, but not as her father. And then comes Ashton, the father who is coming out of nowhere. This is such a big change for her."

I take a deep breath but the tightness in my chest still refuses to leave me. "I hope you're right, Soph. I'm just afraid I'm ruining her."

Sophie squeezes my shoulder lightly. "No. You're not ruining her," she assures me, prompting me to rest my head on her shoulder. "Do you remember eight years ago, when you came home to shock everyone with your pregnancy and your plan to give her away? You were so determined about it, but then you started to fall in love with your little bun. You were so brave during the delivery and raised your baby while you had to finish your study. Honestly, I wouldn't be able to carry on if I were in your position. And look at Chloe, she's now grown into an amazing kid. Because she has an amazing mother."

I listen to Sophie while reminiscing about the time I held Chloe in my arms for the first time. Chloe cried so hard as if she was complaining about how cold and uncomfortable the world was for her, but that was also the moment when I realized how strong mothers felt for their babies. My maternal instincts kicked in and I vowed I would protect her at any cost.

"None of us is a perfect mother. Hell, I even snapped at Diana way more than I should lately. The point is, we are learning to be good mothers. And we are growing into it."

I sigh as I let her words sink. Maybe she's right. I hope she's right.

Days turn to weeks and weeks turn to a month, yet Chloe still doesn't want to have anything to do with Ashton. But she's opening up more lately, especially after she's back to school; she's now also back to her old self. Still, I need to be careful every time I bring up a father-daughter topic in front of her. I'm afraid it will push her back deeper into her hiding hole.

Ashton, of course, has gotten more and more anxious about this slow progress. I know this new role, the daddy role, is a totally uncharted area for him, and he wants to see what he can do about it sooner than later. However, Chloe's refusal throws him to the backseat and forces him to sit tight and wait, while watching me in the passenger seat, guiding Chloe on how to drive the car.

Despite all these roller-coaster emotions we are dealing with right now, I never act differently at work and keep myself under the radar. No one can know my connection with our CEO. It's not that hard because I only see him in the monthly meeting. All I need to do is stare at my feet for the whole thirty minutes to avoid eye contact with him.

The gossip about him and Diandra still goes around —apparently, they have overcome their issue— and people are speculating about him announcing their engagement soon, probably in the annual corporate gala in the summer. It's a popular moment for our executive members to announce important news about their personal lives. And I decided that I'm not looking forward to the event.

But today, Chloe is in a different mood. The school seems to bring back the cheerfulness in her. I can't help stealing glances at her from the rear-view mirror and smile at the sight. And yes, I've decided to bring her myself to school again after the accident. I'm having a trust issue with anyone on the street at this very moment.

"Does Mr. Knight have kids?" she asks out of the blue, making me almost forget to hit the acceleration as the traffic light turns green.

"What do you mean? You are his kid."

"I mean, does he have a wife and kids at his home?"

"No. He doesn't have a wife or a kid at his home." I reply while glancing at her from the rearview mirror. "Why do you ask?"

Chloe shrugs. "Just curious. Maybe I have siblings?"

I scoff inwardly. Ashton didn't even want a kid in the first place. Unless there is another unrevealed broken condom fun fact. "Not that I know." I chew my lower lip, refraining from pushing the topic further.

"Is he a nice person?"

I blink at her question. If I want to make this easier, I can just lie to her and say whatever my daughter wants to hear, but I promised I would never lie to her again. "He is... a unique person. Some find him nice, some don't. But I can assure you that he's a good person. He let you rest and sleep in his office room back then, remember?"

"But is he nice to you? Has he ever made you sad?"

"No, sweetie, your father never made me sad. On the contrary, I made him sad because I didn't tell him about you sooner."

"Why didn't you tell him sooner?"

"Because I was afraid."

"Afraid of what?"

I bite the inner part of my cheek, thinking about how to let her understand the complexion of my fear, but then I decide to go with the simplest way. "Because Mama lied a lot, sweetheart. It's very bad and it makes a lot of people sad."

"Ow." That's the only response she gives me, making me even more curious about what is going on inside her head right now. When our car finally reaches her school gate,

Chloe says lightly, "I think we should invite him to eat dinner with us, maybe it will make him not feel so sad anymore."

Chapter 22

The dinner goes amazingly well. For some reason, I manage to serve the delicious beef Wellington which I've never cooked before. The table is full of different kinds of side dishes, adorned by a pair of decorative red candles and red roses at the base of my mom's classic candelabra. Everyone at the table is smiling warmly, reflecting a perfect little family.

I wish it was real but well, that's the scene in my dream last night. The actual dinner is different. Very different.

I've cooked stuffed chicken breasts, roasted potatoes, steamed mixed greens, and garlic sauce. No candles, no antique candelabra, and no flowers. What we have now is just a plain wooden dining table that is enough to hold all the eating utensils for the three of us. This isn't a dinner to impress; this is a dinner to test.

Despite being the one who came up with the idea, Chloe is pretty reserved and quieter than usual. But thankfully, she isn't totally closed up or worse, showing resentment that can cause drama. I hope it's just her usual phase when we have company she isn't familiar with. She sometimes gets shy but then warms up as time passes by. Her bright green eyes steal glances at Ashton now and then when he doesn't look, but once he turns his gaze to her, she looks down at her plate right away, suddenly busy with her meal.

"You have a very comfy house, Chloe," Ashton says. "How long have you been living here?"

Instead of answering, Chloe shifts her gaze to me. She's never been this timid in front of a house guest before. I nod at her, encouraging her to reply to her dad.

"Since I was two," she says, her little fingers gripping the adult-size fork before sticking it into the potato. Chloe's refused to use children's cutlery since she turned five.

"Oh. Where did you live before?"

"In grandma's house."

"That sounds fun. Did you like it there?"

Chloe frowns. "I can't remember. I was still a baby."

"Right," Ashton mutters under his breath. "So, do you spend holidays at grandma's place a lot?"

Chloe shakes her head. "Not that often anymore."

Ashton raises her eyebrows, showing his interest. "Why not?"

Chloe shrugs. "Grandma says no a lot. No for riding a bike on the street, no for climbing the tree, no for playing with the children in the neighborhood, a lot of no."

"Well, I agree with your grandma about the bike. Riding a bike on the street can be dangerous."

"Ashton hasn't seen grandma's neighborhood," I interject as I see a disagreement scowl forming on Chloe's face. "Of course you can ride your bike on that street."

"Still, there are a lot of reckless drivers on the street nowadays," Ashton mumbles as he slices his chicken.

"Where can she ride her bike if it's not on the street then?" I ask. We haven't got a chance to have the parenting talk since we wanted to wait for Chloe to come around first. As much as I want to discuss it privately, there is something seriously wrong with his knowledge about raising kids that I need to address right here, right now.

Ashton purses his plump lips, making me slightly distracted from the view. "In the park? There's a bicycle path and it's safe for kids."

I give him a deadpan look. "Chloe rides her bike to learn about rules on the street so that she can be more and more mobile and be independent, not depending on her parents all the time. She's almost eight."

"Exactly. She's still seven."

I open my mouth in disbelief. Does he really think that kids don't need to learn through the process and are automatically able to do everything when they are bigger? Was he born as a baby or just being dropped from the sky like Mr. Bean?

Chloe's big eyes look at us back and forth while Ashton and I are having a small argument about where she should ride her bike. For a second, I'm afraid that it will poke her nerves and make her think having a daddy around is a bad idea, but instead, she giggles.

"Do you ride a bike, sir?" she asks with eyes full of curiosity.

"I told you to call me Ashton. And yes, I did when I was a kid."

So, he wasn't dropped from the sky as an annoying adult. Good to know.

"Where did you ride your bike?"

Ashton wrinkles his nose. "In our yard, it was super big, or in the park."

"Never on the street?"

"Well...yeah. I went to school with my bike sometimes," he replies in defeat. "But, things were different back then."

Ah, the ultimate card any parent will pull when they don't know how to explain their reasoning logically to their kid.

"Different how?" Chloe pursues.

"Less traffic, people were friendlier, and" —Ashton purses his lips again, glancing at me with a 'help me' look, which of course, I gladly ignore— "just less dangerous in general." When Chloe tilts her head, trying to make sense of her dad's words, he adds, "But of course, your mom is also right here. As much as it's dangerous riding a bike on the street, you gotta learn at some point."

His last line prompts me to grin, rather smugly, but I hide it behind the napkin I'm using to wipe the non-existence food crumbs around my lips. And of course, the observant Ashton catches this. He glares at me, yet his lips twitch as if he's holding back a smile. And oh, is that an admiration glint that I see in his eyes? I might be imagining it.

If I could choose, I'd rather fix my eyes on the last chunk of chicken on my plate instead of having eye contact with

Ashton. This man still makes my stomach flutter and turns my knees to jelly every time her sharp gaze is fixed on me. I feel like a teenager again, and it's infuriating. But he can't know because this will just add unnecessary drama for all of us. This infatuation will cease eventually; it's just temporary.

"May I ask some questions, si...Ashton?"

"Sure. You can ask me anything." Ashton tears his eyes from me and gives Chloe his full attention.

"How many brothers and sisters do you have?"

"I have one big brother and one big sister."

"Do you live with them?"

"No."

"Do you live with your parents?"

"No. My father has passed away, and my mother lives alone."

"Do you have dogs?"

"No."

"Do you have cats?"

"No, Chloe. I live alone without house pets."

"It must be super lonely," Chloe replies. "But do you have a girlfriend then?"

"Uh, uuuum, I have a close friend, yes."

I'm listening to the conversation quietly while stabbing my last carrot with my fork.

"Are you going to marry your close friend?"

"Uh, whew, getting personal, aren't we?" Ashton laughs in a nervous tone.

"I'm sorry! I thought I could ask anything." Chloe's eyes widen before looking down at her plate again, her cheeks turning pink from embarrassment.

"No, no. It's fine," Ashton corrects himself quickly. "I'm just not used to being... interrogated."

Chloe looks up and her bright eyes meet her dad's. "Okay."

"So, what was the question again? Right, about marrying my lady friend. Hmm, I don't know about that, yet."

I release the breath I don't know I was holding, prompting Asthon to glance at me with a curious look.

"Why not?" Chloe asks.

Ashton reverts his eyes to Chloe, smiling at her. "Because, right now, I'm still busy with something else that I find more important."

"Oh? Are you going to buy a house?"

"No."

"Are you going on vacation?"

"Nope."

"What is more important than getting married then?"

Ashton chuckles before putting his cutlery on his plate. He folds his arms and rests them on the table while fixing his eyes on Chloe. "It's you."

"Me?" Chloe looks genuinely surprised by his answer.

"Yes. I prefer to spend time with you because I would love to know you better."

A faint smile curls up on Chloe's lips. "You do?"

"Yes. And I've been thinking of taking you out sometime on the weekend. Maybe we can go see fish in the Waterworld, or go to the zoo if the weather is nice. And oh, the amusement park also sounds like a good idea. What do you think?"

Chloe's eyes twinkle every time Ashton comes up with the idea of a place they can go together. "Can Mama come?"

Ashton glances at me. "Of course, if she wants to."

All I can do is smile at the pair as I nod, trying to hold back the tears of joy that are beginning to pool in the corners of my eyes. I don't want them to see how easy they make me or break me, because it's not about me. It's about Chloe.

Chapter 23

It still feels surreal seeing Chloe opening up to her father after she refused to see him for a whole month. She's getting more and more curious about what kind of life her old man has. Well, to be truthful, she isn't the only one, but I refrain from being nosey. The less I know about him, the better it is, for my peace of mind. Right?

Since the dinner, Chloe hasn't stopped asking questions about Ashton Knight as if I've known him all my life.

"Can you text him my questions? This is important," begs Chloe when we are driving home from Sophie's house. My sister cooked extra pumpkin soup today and wouldn't let us leave without eating dinner with them.

"Why is it important?"

"Because it is. Pleeease."

She knows she's hitting my soft spot when she gives me that puppy look. I sigh. "Fine. I'll text him when we're home. But he is a busy man, I can't promise he will reply right away."

"It's okay. I still have time. Thank you, Mama," she grins from ear to ear.

"You still have time for what?" I squint my eyes at her. I'm glad I've invested my money in a full rear-view mirror. It comes in super handy when I drive and talk to my kid at the same time.

"I can't tell you yet," she replies as she shakes her head. Judging from the determination on her face, it's no point in pushing further.

As promised, once we are inside our garage, I retract my phone from my bag and text Chloe's dad.

Me: Q#9 What's your fav color? Q#10 What is your fav animal? Q#11 What is your fav food?

"Done," I say as I open the driver's door. "Now, it's bath time, and get ready for bed. We stayed too long at aunt Sophie's today."

"Aye, aye, captain!" she squeals and jumps out of the car before dashing to her room.

Smiling at her cheerfulness, I go straight to the kitchen to do my routine: unloading the dishwasher and bringing the trash out. In the next thirty minutes, I help Chloe dry her hair and put on her pajamas while listening to her ramble about what happened in school today. It's always a wonder to me how she babbles all the time but once I read her bedtime story, her eyelids become droopy all of sudden. By the time I finish reading, she's already snoring softly while cuddling her Galileo plush.

It's already past ten when the text from Chloe's dad pops up on my screen.

Knight, Asston: You've worked for me for a month, yet you can't answer this? Tsk.

Me: I worked to sort out your documents and appointments. Not as your nanny.

Knight, Asston: My bad should've asked you to be my nanny then. Having a hot nanny is every guy's ultimate fantasy.

My eyes bulge when I read his reply. Did he really type this dirty message? I never get the impression of him being a flirty human being. He must be drunk right now. Even though I know I shouldn't take this seriously, I can't help feeling the excitement in the pit of my stomach.

Me: Will you answer, sir? It's for Chloe.

Knight, Asston: Don't call me sir or my mind will go where it shouldn't

Knight, Asston: Blue. Lion. Food.

Me: Your favorite food is food?

Nothing from him for the rest of the night. I'm guessing he has passed out on his bed from his phone knocking his head. I chuckle at the mental image.

This is the first time I witnessed his kinkiness and it makes me feel giddy nonetheless. I'm hot, huh? Was he being honest? No, dumbass. He's a drunk, my logical mind scolds me, and you need to stop grinning like a schoolgirl now.

When I wake up in the morning, the notification from Ashton is blinking on my screen.

Knight, Asston: I mean, I like all kinds of food. I don't have a favorite.

Knight, Asston: And I was intoxicated last night. Sorry for the inappropriate messages. I didn't mean it.

I feel my stomach drop. Of course, he didn't mean it.

Me: I figured :) Don't worry about it.

Knight, Asston: See you two on the weekend. I'll be there at nine.

Chloe agreed to go to a funfair with Ashton only if I would go, too. And of course, I said yes. I know it's going to be weird to go together while we aren't a couple, but I understand why Chloe wants me to come with her. It's her very first time having a daddy day-out, and she's still nervous to be alone with him. Having her mama around is the safest bet if things don't go to plan.

Soon, she will need to learn to bond with her dad without me being present. It's good for them, and also for me. If the three of us spending time together becomes a habit, my attempt to push him out of my mind will be doomed to failure.

The day has been bliss. After the prolonged cold weather, we are finally blessed by the luxury of the late-spring sun. However, Chloe's happy face and laughter are brighter than the sun. We've been jumping from one ride to another ride, stopping at all kinds of booths, and stuffing our faces with snacks while strolling around the funfair. After having an early dinner, we agree to head home with a potato sack full of toys and stuffed animals we won today.

We're completely worn out when we drive home, and none of us is in a chatty mood. The trip is only accompanied by blues music from Ashton's car stereo, occasionally disturbed by Chloe's snoring from the backseat. I can't help thinking that this would've been the life we had if we were a family, if we were a couple. Don't go there, Char. Scolding myself, I heave a sigh while pushing my wandering thoughts to the back of my mind.

When Ashton pulls over in our driveway, Chloe is still asleep in her booster seat.

"I guess I need to carry her upstairs." I chuckle softly.

"Let me," Ashton replies as he unbuckles himself and gets out of the car.

No pajamas, no bath, and no brushing teeth for tonight, but seeing how peaceful her face is right now, I will let her just sleep through the night this time. After pulling up her cover, we quietly walk downstairs.

"Thank you for today," I say as we stand next to his Mercedes Benz. "Chloe and I had a good time."

Instead of opening his door, Ashton leans back against his car, facing me with his hands in his pockets. "No. I thank you for this," he replies. "I was afraid that spending the day with me is some kind of a buzzkill for her, because I have no clue what to do. Luckily, you tagged along."

"She's been waiting for today, though. And you weren't a buzzkill for sure."

"Yet, she wouldn't go if Mama didn't go," Ashton remarks before correcting himself, "but I totally understand that. I'm just hoping it doesn't mean she is afraid of me or afraid to be alone with me."

"Nah, Chloe might have all these bursting feelings about her newfound father, but feeling afraid is none of them. You know, it's always been just the two of us since she was born. She still needs to get used to this."

Ashton nods. "Likewise, this is also new to me."

"How are you holding up by the way?" Mimicking his gesture, I slip my hands into my jeans pocket. "I mean from not wanting to have kids, and now you've got a seven-year-old daughter in one blink of an eye."

"Holding up alright, I guess. Not gonna lie that it scared the shit out of me at the beginning." He chuckles, looking at the ground. "Though the more I learn about her, the more I can see myself in her. But I'm gonna be honest with you, I still don't know what I'm doing now. I've seen how my siblings are with their kids, and that's all I know."

I smile at him earnestly. "Whatever you're doing now, it brings a smile to Chloe's face. So, it's a good thing, isn't it?"

"I hope so." Ashton smiles, not a smirk, not an obliging smile, but the first real smile he's ever given me. "I'm glad that you're Chloe's mother. You're an amazing mom."

I feel the heat creeping up on my face. I've heard this line far too often from other people, but when it's coming from Chloe's father, it gives me the fulfillment that I don't even know I craved for. "Thank you."

I thought it was the last thing he would say before turning around and hopping on his driver's seat, but he stays rooted on his spot, looking down as he crosses one leg over the other. Should I invite him in? No. Keep your distance, keep your distance, keep your distance...

"Can I ask you something personal?" Ashton's voice brings me up to the current moment.

"Depends," I reply carefully, "on how personal it is."

"It's about Watkins."

"Okay?" I hold my breath, waiting for his question.

"How did he...take this? I mean, we spent time together as a family, even though it was only for Chloe. But, is he okay with this?"

I frown, trying to follow where he is getting at. "It doesn't matter if he's okay with it or not, does it? It's not his decision to make."

Ashton chews his lower lip as if he is deciding what to say next. "You didn't answer my question that day, about you and Watkins getting back together. So, I don't know how this whole thing works with the three of us and Watkins, if he's also in the picture."

"What I can say now is, he isn't in the picture. Not after I saw how hard Chloe took all of this in the beginning. My...love life can wait."

My answer seems to surprise him. "Oh."

"What about you?" I ask, looking up at him. "Have you told Diandra about Chloe?"

"I'm about to, but I wanted to ask you first about how we are going to do this. I mean, what if she wants to meet Chloe. Would you permit that?"

Hell, no. "I prefer you and Chloe to get to know each other a bit more before involving someone else. Let her get used to you first, and then maybe meet your family. Not saying Diandra isn't as important as your family, but for Chloe, learning about her family from your side is also a priority right now."

Ashton nods, looking deep in thought. "Got it."

All of a sudden, I feel my energy leave my body, and I don't want to be around him anymore right now. "It's been a long day and I'm tired. You should go home."

Chapter 24

'm in deep shit and I know it.

Instead of wriggling myself out of this unwanted infatuation, I'm attracted to Ashton Knight more and more. My chest is burnt with jealousy every time the man and his lady friend jump into my mind. To make it worse, everyone at work keeps talking about the stunning red-haired woman who shows up more often at our CEO's office lately. The news about Ashton Knight going to tie the knot spreads like a bushfire, but I refrain from asking him about the latest rumor, not that he's going to share his personal life with me anyway.

Since the day we went to the funfair together, Ashton hasn't spent time with Chloe again. He had to leave town in the last two weekends for business trips, and work has been crazy busy as the mid-year is approaching, slapping everyone's faces and reminding us of our annual target. This madness will kick us in the ass until summer vacation begins.

Meanwhile, the corporate gala dinner is also drawing near. I wish I could skip the company annual party but since I'm still a newcomer, I'm expected, scratch that, I'm obliged to attend the gala. Dammit. It's starting to poke my nerves every time the girls gush over the gowns they're planning to wear, which catering is going to serve the meals, which music bands, what decoration theme, and who they are going to bring to the gala.

While the girls are chattering about who's going to be their date, I'm now having the 'Dear John' talk with my potential plus one. I was thinking of asking Ethan to come to the gala with me, but it was before Chloe heard my confession, and it changed everything. For now, I need to stop bringing someone new into Chloe's life. It's been confusing enough for her already.

"So, Chloe hates me now because I left?" Ethan asks while frowning at his coffee.

"Hate is a strong emotion. I don't think that's what she has right now." I run my finger on the edge of the saucer in front of me. "Chloe has been projecting her disappointment for not having her father around, which she thought was you. So, she looked for a reason to hate Ethan Watkins to justify her feelings. I think it's more of her coping mechanism."

"But now she knows I'm not the father. What does this mean to her then?"

"I don't know yet, to be honest. I believe she's still coming to terms with these changes. But the more I think about this, the more I see that she's been bitter because of the absence of her father, not because of you as Ethan Watkins. And my lies mixed everything up." I cover my face with my hands in exasperation. "God, I screwed up big time."

"Hey," Ethan pulls my hands off my face and urges me to look at him. "Don't be too hard on yourself. You did what you thought best at that moment. You didn't know any better."

I sigh. "I swear I wanted to tell her the truth when the time comes. I just didn't expect that you and her dad would swing back into my life at the same time, this soon."

Ethan forces a smile but it doesn't reach his eyes. "Life never stops surprising us, does it?"

"Yeah," I mumble while gripping his hands that are still on mine. "I'm so sorry, Ethan. I wish things worked differently. I was really considering giving us a shot but I can't do that now. Not when Chloe is still confused with everything."

Ethan's eyes turn softer. "Char, I told you I would wait-"

"No," I interject, "please, don't wait. I don't want to promise anything right now. And you need to move on, Ethan."

"I do?" Ethan's voice sounds more like a whisper. He chuckles softly but his eyes betray his gesture. "I don't know how."

"You will figure it out. You always do." I squeeze his hands for the last time before I let them go.

I wasn't lying when I said I considered taking him back. Heaven knows how much I loved him, and how I tried my best to be the girl he wanted back in the day. Dealing with my mom's constant critiques about my choices, Ethan was the only one who understood me. Well, besides Sandy. Being with him is easy and so familiar. Despite the eight years of not having contact with him, it would be easy to fall back in love with him if we kept seeing each other. But being in a relationship isn't my top priority now, especially when my daughter needs her mom during this transition.

History repeats itself. Chloe was the reason he left back then, and now I'm turning him down for the same reason. Only this time, my heart isn't scattered into pieces as I say my goodbye.

The gala night has arrived. After all the hassle in finding the dress, the accessories, and all the necessities, I finally emerge from Sophie's bedroom door, wrapped in an emerald green dress. The girls squeal in unison as Chloe jumps around me and extends her tiny hand to feel the softness of the fabric.

"You look so beautiful, Mama." Her eyes twinkle. "Can I have the same dress too?"

Sophie laughs at the question. "Let me ask the boutique if they can make one for you."

"And for me, too!" Diana says in excitement before walking to me and touching my dress.

"Okay, girls. Hands-off or you're going to ruin Char's dress. Everyone go to the car now! It's time to take princess Fiona to the ball to find her Shrek."

In the next forty minutes, I'm making my entrance into the top floor of the Remington building where they hold the party this year. I have to say I'm in awe of how they've magically changed this floor into a ballroom. Velvet draperies in bordeaux and gold shades blanket the wall, even the ceiling, screaming sophistication, and prosperity. The dancing floor is situated in front of the podium, surrounded by round dining tables that are already partly occupied.

I haven't seen any familiar faces as I walk to my designated table. I know I will not be seated with anyone on my team because this is the idea of the annual party: blending with other employees under the same company group. Deep down, I start to regret not asking anyone to be my plus one. Even bringing Mrs. Donegal's gardener sounds like a good idea now. This is going to be a long night.

"Did you come alone?" asks a red-haired girl who is sitting next to me.

What's up with the world and red hair lately? Why are they everywhere now? I smile at her. "Yes. Not very smart, I know," I reply as I glance at the empty seat next to her. "You're alone, too?"

"No, my partner is," she sweeps the floor with her eyes then shrugs, "somewhere."

I chuckle lightly before offering my hand. "I'm Charlotte."

"Jenny. Pleased to meet you, Charlotte..." Her voice falters as her hazel eyes shift in the direction of the ballroom door. "Oh my. He's really bringing her."

"Who?" I follow Jenny's eyes and regret it right away.

Ashton walks into the room in his black tuxedo, looking terribly handsome as always, with his lady friend wrapping her hand around his arm. She is wearing a gold sequin dress that snugs perfectly on her petite body. The reflection of light on her dress shines blindingly as she moves. Her hair is pulled into a bun and her make-up is done skillfully as if she is prepared to walk on a Hollywood red carpet.

I hear a snort next to me. "She looks like a gold mine."

I turn my head to the grinning Jenny before bursting into laughter with her.

"Sorry, don't mind my sarcastic remark. She's just... phenomenal," Jenny apologizes.

"It's fine. Do you know her?"

"Of course. She used to work here." Jenny's eyes follow the couple that are now sitting at the executive table. "I don't know what makes him want to go back together with her. She's trouble."

"You always say I'm trouble, yet you keep coming back for more," says a deep voice. A man with jet-black hair and mesmerizing deep blue eyes must have sneaked up and sat next to Jenny while we were eyeing Diandra. He gives Jenny a peck on the cheek before turning his gaze to me. "Hello, I'm Blake. Jenny's fiance."

The next hour is all about company achievement, appreciation for the best employees —Jenny is on the list, and some announcements from the executive members. The moment of truth is about to arrive. People on my floor made a bet on Ashton announcing his engagement with Diandra tonight, and they're about to find out who is going to lose money.

When the Chief of Human Resources steps up to the podium to announce his coming retirement, I excuse myself and head to the ladies' room. I feel jittery all of a sudden and can't bring myself to hear the rest of the announcements from the remaining executive members. At least, if Ashton indeed announces his engagement with her, I don't have to see his face.

Staring blankly at the bathroom mirror, I contemplate calling a taxi and heading home. People won't find out, will they? Even if they do, I can always come up with excuses. At least, I showed up, and that is the bare minimum requirement for newbies. My internal debate is disturbed by the swinging door, revealing a woman in a gold sequin dress who is glaring at me.

"We need to talk."

Chapter 25

Too dumbfounded to react, I stare at her from the restroom mirror.

"What kind of game are you trying to pull?" Diandra asks. The mix of sadness and resentment in her eyes sends a chill down my spine. I turn around as she walks toward me slowly like a lion approaching its prey. My figure is significantly taller and more athletic than hers, yet it doesn't intimidate her one bit.

"I beg your pardon?" I reply.

"What is your real intention behind all of this? Do you need money? Or position for your career in this company? Or do you want his last name? Or is it just a fun game for you?"

"I'm not sure I'm following you."

Diandra scoffs. "Please, we don't have time for this. Don't beat around the bush."

"And we don't have time for riddles. If you can tell me what bothers you, then we can maybe find a solution for that."

"You put Ashton in a very difficult position for whatever reason. That's what bothers me. Using your daughter to corner him, really?"

I frown, still stumbling into every word she throws at me. She just doesn't make any sense. "Using my girl to corner him? What are you talking about?"

"Our relationship is stuck because of a daughter that came out of nowhere, begging for his attention."

"I beg your pardon?" My mouth is hanging open, taken aback by her bluntness.

"Very well played. And you knew it well that he's a good man who would never abandon a child who has his blood running in her veins. But don't you think you're taking this too far, Charlotte?"

My fingers clutch the edge of the wash table so tightly that it is almost painful. "Look, I don't know what your problem is and what situation you two are having at the moment, but I know I never cornered him into anything. The only time I forced him to be there was when my daughter needed blood supply. I had no choice. What kind of mother would do nothing when she saw her kid was in danger?"

Her eyes soften in a split second. "I'm sorry you had to go through that."

Instead of replying to her sympathetic line, I cross my arms over my chest, still on full alert, ready for her next blow. This woman has just stormed into this restroom like a whirlwind and accused me of doing something absurd. Has she gone nuts? Or is she high?

Diandra paces back and forth across the room, her heels clicking against the marble tile, echoing painfully in my ears. "You know I didn't blame him or give him the cold shoulder when he told me he had a kid. It just pained me to see how it hit him like a truck. Did you know he never wanted children? And now he's forced to accept reality and take action as any responsible adult should–"

"Again, I never forced him–"

"–yet it wasn't enough for you. You pushed him even further, and now he feels trapped between his obligation to be a father and your demand to cut me out of his new battle."

"What do you mean by my demand to cut you off?"

Diandra stops short and looks me straight in the eye. "You're not letting me meet your child. You" —she points her forefinger at me— "made him choose between me and your daughter. That is low, Charlotte, even for you. You can't stop a man from pursuing a relationship with the ones he cares about, in this case, me and your daughter."

I groan out of frustration. "I never made him choose! That's not my intention at all!"

"We all know he's handsome, rich, powerful, and women want to get their claws into him, you included. But please, get real, this isn't uni life anymore, this is real life that requires maturity. You need to know that your childish attempt to have him for yourself is rather silly."

"Whoa, hold on there!" I raise my hands, ordering her to stop. "I'm not going to stand here and listen to your empty accusations. You don't know what happened, and you'd better shut up before you humiliate yourself!"

"Oh, I know what happened. Ashton told me everything."

"Then you should know that everything I do now is for Chloe. This is a crucial moment for her to learn about the father who was never there in her first eight years of life."

"It's crucial for Ashton, too, you know." When I can't answer her, she continues, "Why not let me help? Why shut me out instead? If you want to make this work between Ashton and his child, then you should also let me in. Ashton needs my support; he needs me." Mirroring my gesture, Diandra crosses her arms over her chest and heaves a sigh. "Honestly, it doesn't feel like you're doing this for Chloe. You're just trying to control his life through your daughter, and that is pathetic."

"I...you know what? This is stupid. Why are we having this conversation in the first place? As far as I know, the problem lies between you and your boyfriend. Go and fix it with him, and leave me out of it. I'm done here." With that, I stomp to the door.

"All I'm asking is your permission to meet his daughter so that I can help him go through this."

My hand freezes on the handle while my eyes stare blankly at the door before me, questioning myself why I don't just walk away right now.

"I'm standing here and asking you, a woman to a woman, would you please at least think about it?" she asks.

As far as I hate being ambushed like this, she probably has her point about Ashton being trapped in a difficult situation. But I don't trust her. But again, I don't know what to think right now. I clench my jaws. "Fine. I'll give it some thought."

"And one more thing. What is said here stays here. He doesn't need to know this because things have been rough already for him lately. This is just between us, and we will handle this like mature adults."

Without saying any more words, I yank the door open and scramble through the corridor to find my way out. My sight has gotten blurry from the tears as I look for the exit sign.

I leave the building after the restroom talk since I don't have the energy to stay at the party any longer.

Diandra might have pointed out the truth about me putting Ashton in a difficult spot, but my heart still refuses to agree to it. If Ashton found this a problem, why didn't he say it to my face? Why did he complain to his girlfriend instead of confronting me? He doesn't strike me as a man who has problems speaking his mind.

But again, learning that he had a daughter all of a sudden must have been terrifying for him. He probably had the inner debate between taking his role as a father or denying us completely. Unfortunately, being a successful man carrying a well-known surname doesn't leave him much choice. He's forced to behave the way society expects him to because it's not about what he wants anymore. It's about his public image.

I know he wants to be careful when it comes to Chloe and me, but I just wish he told me what bothered him instead of saying "got it" that night after the funfair day. I thought he took my answer well.

And how have I become the bad guy here?

Is it wrong to protect my daughter from further confusion? Is it wrong to do what I think is best for my kid? Also, I don't know what kind of person Diandra is since Ashton hasn't introduced her to me. Is she good with kids? What kind of things will she say to Chloe when I'm not present?

I feel like I'm going crazy now.

I take a taxi home without calling Sophie. Chloe is having a sleepover at her house tonight because I'm expected to be home past Chloe's bedtime, and I'm glad that I have the house for myself. I need to be alone right now. I just want to crawl into my hiding place.

Once home, I grab a bottle of wine and my favorite crystal glass, throw myself onto the couch, and turn on the TV. The talk has made my whole body tense and powerless at the same time. Surely, alcohol sounds like a good distraction for now.

Why did I go to the ladies' room during the gala? Instead of dodging Ashton's announcement about his personal life, I got caught in a more painful situation. Ha! Joke on me. If I stayed put at my table, Diandra wouldn't have dared approach me, and I would have been enjoying my luxurious meal and expensive wine right now. Alas, here I am, with my not-so-expensive wine and no food.

After emptying my first glass, the questions bounce back to the surface, swirling in my head. Am I a bad mother? Am I that immature? Am I being unfair to people who care for Chloe? First Ethan, and now Ashton. Am I still the same impulsive and clueless Charlotte who can never see what is best for everyone but herself? Maybe Diandra is right, maybe it's not just about Chloe. Maybe I want to shut her out because I'm jealous. Has my infatuation with Chloe's dad turned me into a selfish human being then?

I'm not sure how many glasses of wine I've downed but magically, the bottle is half empty. Oops, did I drink all of that? "Bad, bad Charlotte!" I cackle after scolding myself loudly, throwing my head backward. I haven't even eaten anything since my late lunch. I'm so going to get drunk.

Propping myself out off my couch, I walk to my home phone and order pizza with a lot of giggles and slurring in my voice, making the lady on the other side almost hang up on me. Once I finish ordering, I lean on the wall, thinking about what I'm going to do but my mind is dwindling, and it's getting harder to think.

It's when the screaming doorbell startles me. Is the pizza delivery here already? How is that possible? Or have I been standing here that long? Wrapped in utter confusion, I stride to the door, yank it open, and my eyes stop at the very man whose existence I'm planning to forget for tonight.

"I noticed you leave the gala and you didn't answer my calls. I got worried that something happened at home," Ashton says.

I giggle again. "Oops, sorry. I haven't checked my phone. Wait, lemme see. Where is my phone?" I turn around to look for my bag. It should be sitting on the side table in the hallway, but it's not there anymore. Does the bag have feet now?

"Charlotte?"

"Sir?"

He squints his eyes at me. "Are you drunk?"

I lift my hand, press my forefinger and thumb together, and move them apart slowly while my eyes are narrowing at them. "A little bit."

"Has something happened?" He frowns, his sharp eyes studying my face.

"Something always happened to me, mister."

"What's wrong? Can I come in?"

Without answering him, I leave the door open while shuffling back to the living room. Ashton closes the door and follows me inside.

"Where is Chloe?"

I throw myself on the couch and lean back on the headrest. It's just getting heavier to hold my head straight. "She's at Sophie's. I have the house for myself now. Enough room to think."

"To think about what?"

"About shit."

"What?"

I shrug before grabbing the remote control. The sound from the TV has become painful in my ears. Has it been this loud from the beginning?

"Is it Watkins?"

I raise one eyebrow before chuckling. "No. It's not him. Flash news: I broke things off with him last week."

Ashton sits next to me without tearing his gaze from mine. "You did?"

I nod lazily. "And you know what? I'm sad that I let him go, but I'm also glad I did it. He was my best friend, my lover, my everything. We were so good together. Since he left eight years ago, I've never been in a serious relationship because if he left me, what chances did I have with other men? I've been trying so hard, you know. I want to be a good person. I want to be good for Chloe, and my family, but everything I did always brought pain to everyone. I hurt Chloe, I hurt Ethan, I hurt myself, and you–"

"Me?" Ashton knits his eyebrows. "I have no idea that you hurt me."

"I did. Trust me, I did." My sight starts to blur again. "I shouldn't have dragged you into this, Ashton. You have a life to live, people to please, needs to fulfill, and I ruined everything the day I came to you to ask you to help Chloe."

"What are you talking about? You ruined nothing. If any-thing, I'm glad you came to me that day." He extends his hand and carefully wipes the tears off my cheek, concern on his face. "Do you want to talk about this?"

After admiring the pair of his emerald orbs, my eyes trail down to his plump lips. "Gosh, why does Chloe's dad have to be so hot?"

"What?"

Oops, did I say it out loud? But the faint smile on his lips makes me care less about what he just accidentally heard. And then I do what I've been wanting to do. I scoot closer to him and crash my lips on his.

Chapter 26

His lips are soft, warm, and inviting, making me wonder why I didn't do this sooner. I don't care if he freezes or kisses me back right now, but his soft groan when my tongue licks the seam of his lower lip confirms that he's enjoying it, too. The next thing I know, his hands sneak around my waist and pull me to him as he deepens our kiss. All the doubts, the questions, and the confusion that have been spinning in my head dissipate into thin air. All I know is our locked lips and our intertwined tongues while our bodies are pressed together.

We break off from the kiss to catch our breath, but his lips keep hovering over mine. I keep my eyes shut as our foreheads lean against each other, feeling his warm breath on my face. As much as I want to see his handsome face right now, I don't dare to open my eyes because I'm afraid that this isn't real; that my intoxicated mind Is just imagining this. And then I feel him smiling against my lips before he closes the gap between us. As our lips move in sync, he cups my face with his hands, holding me in place when he slips his tongue between my lips. And once again, I'm melting in his arms.

The doorbell rings from the hallway, prompting us to pull away, and I whimper inwardly from the absence of his warmth.

"Are you expecting someone?" Ashton asks, half grunting.

"Uh, no, I'm not. Wait, the pizza!" I stand abruptly, but my legs still wobble because of the make-out. I'd topple over if Ashton didn't catch me in time. "I need to find my wallet."

"Just sit. I'll take care of it." Gently, he pushes me back to the couch before getting up and walking to the front door.

My heart is still thumping against my chest, my lips are tingling, and my mind is clouded by the intensity of the kiss we just shared. I slump back to the sofa and close my eyes, listening to him talking to the pizza guy, but I can't make out any word from where I sit now. Then the door is closed, followed by the sound of Ashton's footsteps echoing from the hallway.

It's when the realization comes down on me like a bucket of cold water.

What did I do? Did I just kiss him when I knew he had a girl-friend? I cover my face with my hands and groan. What was I thinking? The fact that his girlfriend talked to me less than three hours ago, begging me to help her with her relation-ship problem, makes me feel like I'm the worst human ever. Plus, Ashton is the father of my child; someone I shouldn't mess around with.

"Are you planning to eat all of this by yourself?" He walks to the living room with two extra large pizza boxes in hand. Did I order that?

"Uh, I guess," I reply, my eyes following the boxes as he puts them on the coffee table. In truth, I don't dare to look him in the eye. The guilt of kissing him is hanging heavily on my heart. "Shouldn't you go back to the gala dinner?"

"I know, but I want to make sure you're fine. And," he says, plopping down on the couch at a respectable distance, "we should talk about what just happened."

"I don't know what I was thinking," I say, putting both my hands over my face. "Hell, I don't know what I'm thinking right now. Fuck. I'm too buzzed. I always do stupid things when I'm drunk." I chuckle awkwardly. "Like the old times. But I promise you, it didn't mean anything. I'm sorry I kissed you."

Ashton leans forward with his elbows pressing on his knees, his eyes on the TV screen. "Okay."

I pull my legs up and wrap my arms around them before burying my face in my knees. "You see, I always screw up. I don't think before I act and then get myself into trouble."

"I kissed you too," Ashton replies, but I can tell his mind is elsewhere right now.

"Ashton," I look up and find his eyes are already on mine. "I swear, the last thing I want to do is to stand between you and Diandra. It's hard enough for you two to make room for Chloe, and I don't want to make things more complicated than it already is."

I've never hated myself as I do now. It feels like I'm drowning in the layers of mistakes I keep on creating. A couple of months ago, I promised myself I would make everything right. I would do better, I would not lie again, and I would think carefully before I take action. And now, this.

"You should tell Diandra about this. Tell her I kissed you or cornered you. Tell her it's my fault. I deserve it," I rattle off and don't care anymore if I even make sense.

"What do you mean?" Ashton asks, raising an eyebrow. "I shouldn't lie about the kiss, but I should lie about kissing you back? Which one is it then? Should I lie or should I not?"

It must be the alcohol that messes up my brain. It takes me a good thirty seconds to comprehend his point. I gasp. "You're going to tell her the truth?"

"Maybe."

"Oh god." I bury my face in my knees again with a dramatic groan. "I'm such an idiot."

"Are you going to tell me why you left the party?" he asks.

Not prepared for a sudden change of topic, I frown. The ladies' room scene flashes through my mind, accompanied by a dull jab in my chest. I shake my head. "No."

It takes him ten seconds before he nods. "Alright then. I should go back to the gala." He stands, wearing his usual stoic expression. "You should eat before it gets cold."

The thought of him leaving me behind and returning to Diandra makes my stomach churn. I want to ask him to stay. The words are hanging on the tip of my tongue, but my gradually sobering mind prevents me from doing so. I bite my lower lip as I hear his footsteps receding down the hallway, followed by the sound of the door being closed gently.

This is one of the longest nights I've ever had. After trying to eat a few slices of prosciutto pizza, my mind becomes clearer every second, as well as the recollection of the shitty evening I've had. I'm tempted to finish the rest of the wine every time my head replays the scene of me throwing myself at Ashton. The urge to erase the memory with more alcohol is strong, but the thought of having a nasty hangover in the morning stops me from doing it. Chloe can't see me like that.

At least I'm thinking about the consequences this time.

But I can't sleep. My freaking head just refuses to shut down even though I've been closing my eyes forever. I've counted sheep, I've counted backward, I've counted sheep that are walking backward, still, my brain is as awake as my muscles. This is outrageous.

I sit up straight and extend my hand to turn on the light before glancing at the alarm clock on my nightstand. I hope it's at least 3 AM already so that I have a reason to go to the kitchen and make an early coffee. To my sorrow, it's not even one o'clock yet. How will I get through the night?

Maybe I should sneak into Sophie's house and snuggle next to Chloe. Her snoring always does magic on my sleepless nights.

I scramble out of bed and get dressed. While slipping into my oversize red hoodie, my mind jumps back to the man I should block from my brain for the rest of the night. I wonder if he has told Diandra about the kiss, or if he's going to wait for the right time, or if he's not going to tell her at all. The more I think about it, the more nervous I become.

I start my car as I wait for the garage door to fully open. When I'm about to hit the accelerator, my eyes catch another car parking in my driveway, blocking my way out. The black Mercedes Benz. Pulling back the stick to neutral gear, I jump out of my car before walking tentatively to the car I've grown familiar with.

The driver's door is pushed open, revealing the man who just left my house several hours ago, leaving me with a whirlwind of emotion. Ashton isn't wearing his tuxedo this time. His white dress shirt is wrapped in a black vest that matches the color of his pants.

"Ashton? What are you doing here this late?"

"I saw your bedroom light was on, so I thought I would wait here."

"Still, it doesn't explain why you are here, in this neighborhood."

He closes his door and leans on it. "I ended things with Diandra."

Chapter 27

I can't believe my ears. I stop dead in my tracks, not daring to move, not even breathing. I'm almost convinced this is a dream, and that counting the backward sheep actually worked. Then he walks slowly in my direction. The crunch of the gravel under his shoes, his familiar scent as he moves closer, and his smile —the sad smile, yet the glint in his eyes reflects relief— assure me that this is real.

"Are you alright?" My voice comes out as a whisper.

He nods. "I will be." His eyes graze down to check my attire. "Where are you going this late?"

"I can't sleep. I thought I would just go to Chloe and snuggle with her."

Ashton's eyes turn softer. "Oh, okay. I don't know why I drove here. I can come back tomorrow."

"No, I don't need to go. I would probably wake her up if I went there anyway." I shrug as I cross my arms against my chest, feeling the chilly midnight wind. "Let's go inside."

We go through the garage which has direct access to the kitchen door. I flinch when realizing that I haven't had a chance to clean up. The pizza box is sitting on the countertops, next to the used dishes from our quick afternoon lunch, while Chloe's magazine and pink mug are occupying the dinner table.

"Beer?" I offer after quickly clearing the trash and dirty dishes off the kitchen counter.

"No, I don't think alcohol is a good idea for now. Can I have coffee instead?"

"Sure. I might need one, too."

"No extra sauce, please."

I open my mouth, wanting to answer him, but then I bite my lower lip as I chuckle. "About that, I'm sorry. I was pissed at you and wanted you to pay for the crude remarks you made on my first day."

"Such an interesting choice to punish your boss," Ashton replies, sauntering over to me before leaning back against the counter, and watching me setting up the coffee machine. "I was such an ass that evening; not having a good day at all. But not gonna lie, if I look back at that moment, I always find it hilarious. You were the weirdest yet the most fearless woman I ever bumped into."

"Wow, I'm not sure if it's a compliment but...thanks?"

"You're welcome."

As the machine starts brewing, the silence between us slips in, but it's nothing awkward; it's comfortable silence. The gurgling noise from the coffee machine fills the air while I'm watching the black liquid dripping into the carafe.

"How was the rest of the party?" I ask.

"Good. It went well. People were already going crazy when I got there. You should see Max and the girls on your team. They really killed it." Ashton shakes his head while chuckling.

"Oh, I missed out on the good part."

"There will be an official video for tonight's party. You can see it there." Ashton slips his hands into his pockets, looking down at my kitchen floor while his expression grows darker. "Diandra and I left a little hour after the real party began."

I hold my breath. This must be the part where he had a painful breakup with her. "I'm sorry for what happened between you two."

"Me too. But I know that our...whatever we had was bound to end eventually."

It takes my whole self-restraint to not ask him why it's bound to end because it's none of my business. Still, I need to know whether or not the kiss was one of the reasons.

"Did you...tell her?"

"Well," Ashton starts and then pauses to think, sending my anxiousness through the roof, "I told her I was here with you."

"So, she got mad because of what happened and what I did. And I made you a cheater. Gosh." I bring my hands to cover my face. "This is all my fault. You know what, I can talk to her, I'll apologize and explain that–"

"Stop, Charlotte. Just stop, please," Ashton cuts me. "Stop thinking like you are bad luck for everyone because you are not." Ashton might not raise his voice, but his tone roars the authority that shuts me up at once. "It's not because of you.

The whole situation we've been having is just not healthy anymore. I've been thinking about ending it for some time, and I believe this is the best decision for me and her, and the rest of us."

The machine has stopped making noise, but my mind is too busy hanging on Ashton's every word. When he nudges my shoulder and points at our coffee, I grab the carafe and pour the contents into a pair of Disney mugs.

"Thank you." He takes the mug from my hand and brings it to his lips, inhales it, and carefully sips it. "Diandra and I were a couple a few years back," he continues.

"I heard the story."

"You did?" He glances at me, raising one eyebrow.

I nod. "She was your big brother's executive assistant in Knight and Co., but you weren't the CEO back then. After some commotion involving your brother, she resigned but you kept seeing her before she gradually disappeared from the picture. And she came back recently to reclaim you."

Ashton stares at me with a look I can't decipher. "That was quite a recap of my sad life. I'm surprised you've learned all of this."

"People talk, you know."

He chuckles as he shakes his head. "I bet. But I didn't know that my love life was also interesting for them. I thought they only talked about me because they wanted me dead or something."

I can't help laughing at his comment. "That also."

After our little laughter dies down, he goes on. "We were seeing each other for quite a while but there was always something in the way, something we never agreed on. She wanted children but I didn't. We then broke up because we couldn't see the future the same way."

"Oh, no. And the fact that you have a kid now must be a big slap for her."

He nods. "It is," he replies with a sigh. "When we reconnected again, she said that she finally accepted the fact she would not have kids."

"What do you mean? She gave up her dream of having kids for you?"

"No. She can't have kids. She has an infertility issue." Ashton's explanation sends a dull jab in my gut as if I can feel Diandra's pain. "Then Chloe made her entrance into my life."

I'm speechless. For the whole two minutes, I don't know what to say or what to do. I left the party hating that woman with every fiber in my body, but now my chest is tightening for her. She's been through all this pain, and now she has to learn about another woman who had her future husband's child, a child she can't have. And the fact that I didn't let her have access to Chloe must have made her feel like an outcast.

"She took the news about Chloe hard. She resented me for having a kid with you, she resented Chloe for showing up at the wrong time, but what she resented the most was our decision to not bring Chloe to her yet. She felt left out, and it was how things between us went downhill."

"I don't get it," I mumble, more to myself. "She said she was fine with Chloe in your life."

"She said that? To you? When?"

Oh shit! I shouldn't have said it out loud, but his boring eyes into my skull give me no choice but to tell him the truth. "I talked to her tonight at the party."

Ashton furrows his eyebrows, his tone dangerously low. "Okay?"

"She just asked me, nicely, to let you introduce her to Chloe." Well, that's almost the truth.

"It can't be nicely if you were home and drunk an hour later. I want to know, Charlotte, what exactly she said to you."

I put my cup on the countertop and sigh. "She said that I put you in a difficult situation because I made you choose between her and Chloe. It's cruel considering this is the time you need her support the most. She said that I was breaking you apart because of my immature decision."

Ashton closes his eyes and lets out an exasperated breath. "And you let her words go straight to your head."

"Yeah." I put both my hands on the back of my neck while looking down at the floor. "I couldn't help it. I was just confused, you know, and lost. I still am. I've been doubting myself if I'm a good mom for Chloe, if I know what's best for people who care for her." And once again after so many times tonight, my tears pool in the corners of my eyes. I blink rapidly to prevent them from falling.

"You are a great mom, Charlotte. The best I have seen so far. Even my mom can't hold a candle to you," Ashton says. "And what Diandra said is not true. You're not breaking me apart, not even close. I understand every single decision you made for Chloe and I'm totally on board. I told her that it was our decision to keep Chloe in the family for now, and that she needed to wait if she wanted to be a part of my daughter's life."

I know this situation is painful for Diandra, but I can't help feeling the warmth sneak up in me when I hear his explanation. He does care about Chloe.

"And then she started to rant over this decision we made. She believed that you were trying to control me through Chloe, and that I became a weak man who didn't know what he wanted." Ashton's jaws clench. "I know damn well what I want, and I don't need a woman to tell me what to do. And tonight, enough is enough."

"I'm sorry," I murmur.

Ashton just shrugs and continues drinking the rest of his coffee. "And I'm sorry about Watkins, too. Well, for my selfish reason, I'm glad that he's out of the picture completely now."

A smile sneaks up on my lips when I hear his remark. He sounds more like a jealous man instead of a concerned father. At least, I know that we have this mutual attraction for each other because I can tell by the way he kissed me back.

The kiss.

I wince when the scene of me crashing my lips on him flashes in my head. "Right. We need to talk about the kiss," I say, taking a deep breath to prepare myself for the coming embarrassment. "I'm not gonna lie that you are an attractive man–"

"Oh yeah, I still remember you said it out loud." He laughs but when he sees my deadpan look, he stops. "Sorry."

"But at the moment, my priority is Chloe. I don't want to add extra drama to this. I mean, we just met–"

"We met eight years ago."

"Yeah okay, but we started to get to know each other recently. If we rush into this...you know, the physical attraction between us, I don't think it's a wise thing to do. If we screw up, Chloe's happiness is on the line. My point is that we are still in the phase of getting to know each other, the three of us. And maybe we can take this slow and see what happens?"

Ashton fixes his gaze on me and I suddenly don't know where to look. I sip on my coffee while waiting for his answer, and it feels like forever. His furrow slowly disappears, and a faint smile curls up in the corners of his lips. "I agree."

Nodding, I smile back at him, not sure if this is what I want to hear at the moment, but this is what we should do. I know I will fall deeper every day for the very man who is standing in front of me right now, and it's going to be darn hard to suppress my feelings. But at least we agree we do this for Chloe, our daughter.

"What now?" His deep voice brings me back to the current moment.

I grin at him. "Let life surprise us."

Epilogue

It's still six in the morning but Ashton and I are already sitting in Sophie's kitchen, waiting for Chloe to wake up. After our midnight talk, we decided to hop in his car, drove around, and had some more talk. Well, it was more bantering about what we can or we can not do as parents. Ashton's knowledge about parenting is so much better than the first time she met Chloe at work that day. At least, now he knows that children talk back when he gives them instructions.

"I can't believe that you two haven't got any sleep," Sophie shakes her head as she places two mugs of coffee in front of us which we greedily devour the second she lets go of the handles. She is eyeing us with concern. "Don't you two need to nap before driving back? I don't think it's safe for Chloe."

"Mama?" Chloe croaks as she emerges from the kitchen door and throws herself to me.

"Good morning, sunshine. How did you sleep?" I ask as I wrap my arms around her small figure, burying my face in the crook of her neck under her jaw. The mix of her scent and her night sweats is the best part of my morning routine.

"Good," she replies but her eyes are fixed on the man who is sitting next to me.

"Morning," Ashton greets.

"Morning," Chloe mumbles on my chest. "Is Ashton your Shrek, Mama?"

Ashton raises one eyebrow. "Am I supposed to be Shrek?"

Chloe's eyes trail down to Ashton's torso. "You can, but that's not Shrek's vest."

"Oh. And which one is Shrek again?" Ashton asks.

"Uh oh. Wrong question."

Right after I say it, Chloe jumps off my lap and grabs Ashton's hand before pulling him to the living room. "Come, I'll show you which one."

"Have fun!" I shout at the two as they disappear into the hallway.

Sophie giggles before turning herself to face me. "So, what happened at the party? I thought he had a date, how did you two end up hanging out together?" she asks, half whispering.

"It's a long story, but he broke up with his girlfriend," I reply, mimicking her tone. "I'll tell you the whole story later."

"Can't wait!" she says giddily. "Now, pancake or omelet?"

"Pancake, please," I murmur as I lay my head on the breakfast table. Seems like the coffee fails to do its job this time. The sound of cooking utensils clanking and clinking has turned into a lullaby for me.

I hear Chloe's faint voice not long after, complaining about her dad snoring while the Shrek movie is still playing, followed by Sophie mumbling something to her. The next thing I know, Sophie's hand is on my hair.

"Go to my room, Char."

Ashton can't stay after he drops us home. There is a situation at work that needs his immediate attention. This is also something Chloe has to get used to. Unlike her mama who is always home with her during weekends, her dad is another species on the planet. His working hours are infinite.

After her father's departure, Chloe runs to her room and says she wants to take a nap. But when I walk past her room, I hear soft sobs coming from her room. I stop short and press my ear against her door. Chloe's sniffle is unmistakably clear.

"Chloe? What happened? Can Mama come in?" I ask, answered with her loud moan.

I open her door slightly and stick my head inside to see what's going on. My daughter is sitting on the floor with her open bag between her thighs. Her hand is clutching a... bowl? No, it looks like a coffee mug but it's already split in two. It's not ours because I can't remember we have a blue mug with writing on it.

I walk closer and sit down next to her, softly touching her shoulder which is shaking from crying. "Sweetie, why are you crying?"

"I ruined it, Mama!" Chloe replies between her sobs. "I ruined everything!"

"What did you ruin? The mug? Whose mug is that?"

Instead of answering, Chloe wails harder and throws herself at me. I stop pushing her with more questions and wrap my arms around her small posture to calm her down. Slowly, I take the mug she's been holding and examine it.

The writing on the mug turns out to be a drawing. Chloe's drawing. I can see a part of a Lion's face with an enormous mane drawn in blue marker. When I pick up the other half of the broken mug, it has the rest of the Lion's face and its hand holding a colorful lollipop. I recognize Chloe's handwriting under the candy: Papa.

She made this for Ashton.

Now I understand why Chloe urged me to ask Ashton about his favorite animal, color, and food. Well, it seems like Chloe has decided on the food part for her father.

"Did you break it by accident?" I ask softly.

"Yeah." She nods while sniffling on my chest. "I saved money to buy the mug and the Sharpie paint markers. I wanted to give it to Ashton tonight but I ruined it, Mama!"

"Hey, don't worry, we can make another one, okay?"

"We can't. I don't have an extra mug."

"We can buy some more maybe?"

Chloe wipes off her tears with her tiny hand. "I need to wait then. I don't have enough money to buy it now. It's an expensive one."

"Uh, okay," I murmur as I glance at a piece of a ceramic blue mug with a grey handle in my hand. "Maybe I can help with the money?"

Chloe shakes her head. "It's his gift from me. Not from you."

"I see. What if I lend you money? And you can pay me back in terms. How about that?"

Chloe seems to consider my offer. She looks down at the mug in my hand, hiccuping from the cry before her green eyes are on me again. "Okay."

"I will deduct it from your weekly allowance but you will still have some money to buy other things you like. Sounds good?"

A grin grows slowly on her face before she bobs her head firmly. "Let's make another one tomorrow."

After lunch, I take Chloe to the playground in the nearest park. Even though I have my book in my hand, my mind keeps jumping back to the writing on the mug Chloe has made: Papa. Then a gush of warmth floods my heart. I don't know when she will actually call him that, but I'm not going to push it. She will do it when she's ready.

The vibration in my pocket pulls me out of my bubble of thoughts. I fish my phone out and check my screen. Speaking of the devil!

Chloe's dad: When can Chloe and I go public? After your probation?

Me: I'm not sure. Maybe a bit later.

Chloe's dad: Why?

Me: I told you. I don't want people to associate me with you, and think I'm getting this job because of you. I need to prove myself to them first. I need to nail this big client first. Give me 3 months.

Chloe's dad: 2 months is more than enough to close the deal.

Me: 4 months

Chloe's dad: What? Why does it matter if people talk anyway? They do that all the time.

Me: 5 months.

Chloe's dad: Come on!

Me: 6 months

Chloe's dad: That's Christmas!

Chloe's dad: Okay, okay! Take all the time you need. Geez, woman.

Me: Bingo.

"Mama!" Chloe shouts, prompting me to look up. The girl is sitting on the top of the climbing net with two other kids, waving at me gleefully. And I wave back.

Chloe's dad: I'll bring dessert tonight.

Me: Remember, no kiwi for Chloe. She's allergic to it.

Chloe's dad: Yes, ma'am.

I have to say, I love this side of Ashton. He may be clueless, but he's willing to learn. He may be pushy, but he knows where to stop. And it's more than enough for us to build our little family. I know that we will keep arguing from time to time, or we will keep pushing each other's buttons here and there, but it doesn't matter.

Because we are family, and that's all that matters.

www.ingramcontent.com/pod-product-compliance
Lightning Source LLC
Chambersburg PA
CBHW070940190726
48292CB00004B/1279